D1101185

'Ah, there you are. That was quick. I didn't expect you to get here quite so fast.'

A strangely familiar male voice reached Sophie from across the room. She turned to see who was speaking, and immediately the breath caught in her lungs. All at once her throat was unexpectedly tight.

'Lucas,' she said, her blue eyes widening. A prickle of awareness ran down the length of her spine. He was the devil incarnate, as fiendishly good-looking as ever, with glittering grey eyes that held her fast and right now were registering every bit as much surprise as her own. 'I didn't realise—I mean, I hadn't expected to see you here,' she added under her breath.

Her voice must have had a salutary effect on him, because he seemed to snap out of his stunned reverie and his mouth curved faintly in acknowledgement. 'That goes for me, too, Sophie,' he responded huskily.

Dear Reader,

Christmas… It's that wonderful time of year when families get together to celebrate a very special day. With any luck there might be snow on the ground outside, and children will be playing on their sledges or throwing snowballs at one another, while inside there is a warming fire, and people are making the most of a joyful family gathering.

All those good things are what I wanted for Sophie in this book, A COTSWOLD CHRISTMAS BRIDE.

Things are not going smoothly for her, though, and Christmas promises to be a bleak and lonely time at Woodvale Farm.

Until Lucas comes along, that is. He doesn't know how he's going to do it, but it's up to him to turn things around and help her see that they can have that fabulous Christmas and share a glorious future together.

Happy Christmas to all of you!

Love

Joanna

A COTSWOLD CHRISTMAS BRIDE

BY
JOANNA NEIL

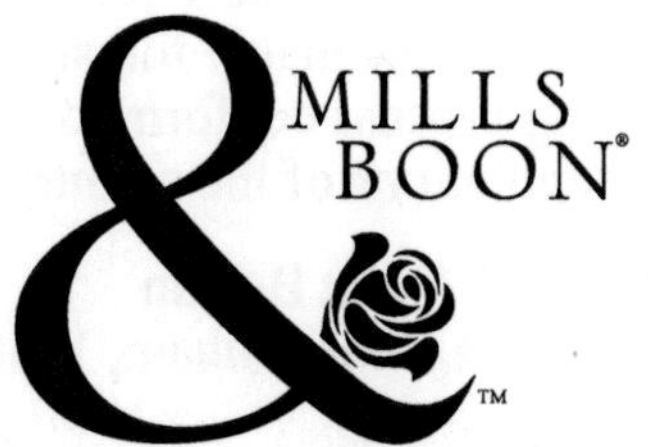

All the characters in this book have no existence outside the imagination of the author, and have no relation whatsoever to anyone bearing the same name or names. They are not even distantly inspired by any individual known or unknown to the author, and all the incidents are pure invention.

First published in Great Britain 2011
by Mills & Boon, an imprint of Harlequin (UK) Limited.
Large Print edition 2012
Harlequin (UK) Limited, Eton House,
18-24 Paradise Road, Richmond, Surrey TW9 1SR

ISBN: 978 0 263 22444 3

Harlequin (UK) policy is to use papers that are natural, renewable and recyclable products and made from wood grown in sustainable forests. The logging and manufacturing process conform to the legal environmental regulations of the country of origin.

Printed and bound in Great Britain
by CPI Antony Rowe, Chippenham, Wiltshire

When **Joanna Neil** discovered Mills & Boon®, her lifelong addiction to reading crystallised into an exciting new career writing Medical™ Romance. Her characters are probably the outcome of her varied lifestyle, which includes working as a clerk, typist, nurse and infant teacher. She enjoys dressmaking and cooking at her Leicestershire home. Her family includes a husband, son and daughter, an exuberant yellow Labrador and two slightly crazed cockatiels. She currently works with a team of tutors at her local education centre to provide creative writing workshops for people interested in exploring their own writing ambitions.

Recent titles by the same author:

THE TAMING OF DR ALEX DRAYCOTT
BECOMING DR BELLINI'S BRIDE
PLAYBOY UNDER THE MISTLETOE
THE SECRET DOCTOR

CHAPTER ONE

'SOPHIE...just listen to me for a minute, please... that's all I'm asking. At least give me a chance to explain...' Nathan's hazel eyes pleaded with her, his hand swooping to grasp her bare arm lightly, and for a second or two, swayed by his obvious suffering, Sophie almost wavered. Almost, but not quite.

She closed her eyes briefly. It was hot in the hotel's ballroom and her head was aching. She couldn't think straight.

In the background the band was playing a heavy rock number, and the noise drummed inside her head. She could feel the vibrations coming up from the polished wooden floorboards, reverberating throughout her body and adding to the tension that was building up in her. At the centre of the dance floor, the happy bride and groom were living it up, surrounded by friends and family.

It was an autumn wedding, but the weather had served them well, with golden bursts of sunshine throughout the day. Now, in the evening, disco lights replaced the sun's rays and cast vivid splashes of colour over the throng. For a fleeting moment as she watched the couple, Sophie longed for just a taste of that sweet, unfettered contentment.

But it wasn't going to happen, was it? Not for her. Not now. She looked at Nathan, her expression strained. It had turned out he wasn't the quite the man she had thought him to be. She'd thought they'd had so much going for them, but in the end all her dreams had come crashing down.

She shook her head. 'I'm sorry, Nathan, I think we've said all we need to say. It's over between us. You have to learn to accept it.'

'I can't do that.' He tugged on her arm, drawing her towards him, and she resisted, trying to pull away.

'Let go of me.' The words came out on a sharp breath of air, and she frowned as his grip tightened on her arm. All evening she'd been trying to avoid him, afraid that this might happen.

She tried to pull herself free once more, but he was more determined than ever, and Sophie began to feel uneasy, not knowing what to do.

'I believe she asked you to let her go.' The man's voice intruded on them, deep and compelling, laced with an inherent thread of authority. It took Sophie unawares, and she turned her head to see who had come to her rescue.

The stranger's grey eyes were focussed directly on Nathan, a warning glint flickering in their steely depths, and as Sophie studied his perfectly etched features, she realised that she'd seen him before, earlier in the day, carrying out his duties as best man at the wedding. Lucas, that was his name. He had jet-black hair and a strong jawline, and he wasn't a man that you would forget easily. He'd made a speech that was full of good humour and positive vibes towards the two young doctors who had just been married. Now, as then, he stood tall and lean, his muscular frame enhanced by the immaculate, expensively tailored suit he wore.

Nathan's fingers remained securely on her arm. 'This is a private matter,' he said, his manner terse and dismissive. 'We don't need any input from you.'

'It seems to me that the young lady doesn't share your view.' Her rescuer kept his voice neutral, but there was a definite threat underlying his words. 'I hope for your sake that you don't want to argue the point with me.' He looked Nathan up and down. 'If you don't release her and walk away from here, I'll be forced to remove you myself. Do you really want to cause a scene?'

Nathan finally appeared to be having second thoughts. Perhaps he took on board the unyielding purpose in his opponent's glittering gaze, or maybe it was the breadth of those shoulders that gave him pause, along with the hint of controlled strength that no amount of trappings could disguise…whatever the reason, Nathan suddenly didn't seem quite so sure of himself. Cautiously, he released his grip on her, and took a step backwards.

'Good,' Lucas said. 'I'm glad you managed to see sense.' He turned his back on Nathan and laid a hand gently beneath Sophie's elbow, leading her away from the edge of the crowded dance floor towards the buffet table. 'It's Sophie isn't it? I'm Lucas. I hope you didn't mind my interruption but you seemed to need a way out of that situation. Now, can I get you something to eat?' he asked.

Sophie shook her head. Right now she couldn't manage to eat a morsel. It was as though her throat was clogged and there was a tight band of pressure around her head. 'No, thanks.'

'Maybe a drink, then?'

'Yes, that would be good.'

'It looks as though pink champagne is the order of the day.' He smiled. 'Would you like a glass?'

She nodded, and waited as he gave the bartender their order. For himself, he chose an ice-cold lager, and after handing her a fluted glass he said softly, 'Here's to new beginnings.'

Her eyes widened a fraction. She was all out of new beginnings. She was wary, guarded against getting involved ever again. But she clinked glasses with him, all the same. 'New beginnings,' she said, and took a sip of the cold liquid. 'I want to thank you for what you did for me, back there. Nathan's a good man, but he's not been himself lately, and I wasn't altogether sure how to handle things. I'm glad that you came along.'

'It was my pleasure.' His glance drifted over her, trailing over the shimmering golden hair that fell in soft waves to rest on her bare shoulders, and then moved on to trace the line of the silk dress that faithfully outlined her slender figure. 'It means I get to be with the most beautiful woman in the room.'

He studied her once more, making her all too conscious of the way the softly ruched material of the bodice clung to her breasts and showed off her narrow waist and emphasised the gentle swell of her hips. From the dropped waistline the skirt was delicately layered, falling to mid-calf. 'The colour suits you,' he said. 'It reflects the blush of your cheeks. You're all peaches and cream… perfect. The bride must have been glad to have you as her chief bridesmaid.'

Hot colour swept along her cheekbones. He was flirting with her, being outlandishly flattering, and she ought to tell him that he was wasting his time but she stayed quiet. She wouldn't be seeing him again after today, so what did it matter?

'You must be a good friend of Harry's?' she remarked, glancing towards the bridegroom, who was still having fun with his new bride on the dance floor. 'He chose you as his best man, so I guess you must have known one another for some time.'

'That's right.' He nodded. 'We grew up together in the same village, here in Buckinghamshire. Of course, we've both moved away since then, but we've always been good friends.' He sent her an oblique glance. 'Do you live locally?'

'No.' She shook her head. 'I booked into the hotel for the night so that I wouldn't have to drive home in the early hours. And, of course, it means that I can have a drink without worrying.'

He nodded. 'That was a sensible decision—though you don't seem to be having all that great a time. I've been watching you and you seem a touch on edge. Is that purely because of Nathan?'

'I suppose so.' Her blue eyes clouded. She wasn't going to confide in him all the things she had on her mind. He was a stranger. A charming, persuasive and thoughtful stranger, but all the same he was not someone she could open her heart to. 'I should have known he would be here. He knows both the bride and groom.'

'He obviously has very strong feelings for you. Had you been together long?'

'About a year.' She finished off her pink champagne. 'We met when he came to look at one of the animals on my parents' farm. He's a vet, and he treated one of the horses that had gone lame. Now it's as good as new.'

'That must have been a great relief for you.'

She nodded, and he took the champagne glass from her, signalling to the barman to fill it up again. 'So you got together, and then things went wrong?'

That hunted feeling caught up with her once more, so that her stomach clenched and she wondered how long it would be before she could escape to her room. 'Yes...only now he won't let go.'

The corners of his mouth turned upwards. 'I can't say I blame him for that. I think I would feel much the same way.'

He handed her a second glass of champagne and she watched the bubbles fizz and sparkle.

The air in the room was hot and oppressive, and she had a raging thirst. She put the glass to her lips and swallowed, feeling the effervescent sting as the liquid coursed down her throat. She felt as though she couldn't breathe, as though the room was closing in on her.

'It looks as though the bride and groom are getting ready to leave,' he murmured. 'Perhaps we ought to say our goodbyes to them?'

She nodded, putting down her empty glass and allowing him to lead the way across the room to the main doors. Lucas pinned back one of the doors so that the bride and groom could slip out and head for their waiting taxi. Sophie tilted her face to the waft of cool air, taking comfort in the brief respite.

They waved off the happy couple, and then had to battle their way through a small crowd of people in order to get back into the ballroom. A wave of heat and dizziness overcame her, and her legs seemed to buckle under her. She fumbled for a handhold on the shelf against the wall, but Lucas was already reaching out for her, supporting her in strong arms.

'Are you feeling faint?' he asked.

She nodded, unable to speak just then, and he turned her towards the foyer. She was content to let him take over. For some reason, her body felt like lead, and her head was muzzy, her brain fogged. In the far reaches of her consciousness, she heard him say something about finding her keys, but she wasn't in any state to answer him. It was strange, having to rely on him like this. She had always been so fiercely independent, but right now she was glad that he was there to help her, because there was no way she could have managed by herself.

They must have gone up in the lift, because she vaguely remembered being still, her body resting against Lucas, her cheek buried in the fine worsted fabric of his jacket. There was a gentle bump as the lift came to a stop and he wrapped his arm more closely around her in order to stop her from falling.

She didn't recall any more of what happened after that. Blackness closed in on her, and there was instant peace, nothingness.

When she came round, some time later, she

was aware of a wonderful feeling of coolness. The fever had left her, and Lucas must have laid a cold, damp cloth across her forehead, because she felt its soothing touch, drawing the heat from her.

Slowly, she opened her eyes. 'I'm in my room?' she asked softly.

'That's right. I found your key in your bag.' Lucas came to her side, gazing down at her, a small line etched into his brow as he studied her. 'Just lie still,' he murmured, when she would have tried to sit up. 'Take your time.' He sat down beside her on the wide bed, looking into her eyes. His very presence was a comfort to her. He appeared so strong and capable, as though he would have no trouble resolving any problem that came his way. 'You passed out.' His mouth made a straight line. 'I was worried about you for a while there.'

'I remember I was dizzy…but I feel so much better now.' She removed the cloth from her forehead and placed it on the bedside table. She gave him a weak smile. 'It looks as though I have to thank you all over again for taking care of me,' she said softly. 'If it hadn't been for you, I might have made a fool of myself back there, collapsing in the ballroom for all to see. I'm sure everyone would have imagined I'd had way too much to drink.' She frowned. 'Perhaps I did.' Would two glasses of pink champagne have that effect on her? You couldn't count the toast to the bride and groom, could you? After all, that had been hours ago. And she'd nibbled some food in the meantime.

'Somehow, I doubt that was the problem.' His voice was a low, warm rumble of sound. 'You looked as though something was wrong, way before you fainted.'

She blinked and stared up at him. Exactly how long had he been watching her? He had turned up at just the right moment to save her from an awkward situation, and that couldn't have happened by chance, could it? And now she was alone with him in her hotel bedroom, and it began to dawn on her that she was becoming increasingly vulnerable, lying here this way and allowing him to make all the running. She didn't know the first thing about him.

She tried to sit up, and suddenly realised that she had complete freedom of movement, with no tight-waisted silk dress to bind her rib cage or folds of soft material to tangle with her limbs.

'Stay where you are for a bit longer,' he advised in an even tone, laying a hand lightly on the smooth, bare flesh of her arm. 'If you try to get up too soon you may become dizzy all over again.'

A ripple of heat ran through her. His gentle, but firm, touch set her heart racing and she looked away from him, away from the purposeful silver glint reflected in his eyes.

Instead, she stared down at bare limbs, at her long, shapely legs, which were naked but for a shimmer of lace that edged her flimsy, silk chemise. She gasped. 'You took my dress off me,' she said in a shocked whisper. Her hand went up to cover the creamy swell of her breasts, but it was a futile gesture, one that came far too late, because he had already seen everything he wanted, hadn't he?

His gaze moved over her, amusement lurking in the depths of his grey eyes. 'I did,' he agreed.

'I thought it was the best course of action at the time. You were burning up, and I thought you might be able to breathe better for being unzipped.'

'But you...you don't know me, and yet you... I can't believe that you would do that...' She stared at him, her blue eyes troubled, her cheeks hot with mortification. 'You could have just undone the zip...that would have been enough.'

'I don't believe in half-measures...and really, you shouldn't worry—I had your interests at heart. I didn't intend to take advantage of you. I didn't mean to embarrass you.'

'But you did.' She fumbled around for a sheet, desperate to cover herself, but she was lying on the duvet and he was pinning it down with the weight of his body so that her efforts were futile.

He shrugged. 'You're worrying too much.'

'That's easy for you to say. I'm not used to being in this sort of situation.'

He gave a half-smile. 'That goes for the two of us.'

She scrambled to a sitting position and then

leaned back as a wave of dizziness threatened to swamp her once more.

Lucas leaned forward and piled up the pillows behind her. ‘See?’ he said. ‘Didn’t I tell you that would happen? Sit back for a while and let the blood settle.’ He assessed her thoughtfully. ‘Seriously, you don’t have to worry about me looking at you. I’m a doctor. My intentions are perfectly honourable, I can assure you of that.’ He left her for a moment and walked to the bathroom.

Returning, he handed her a satin kimono. ‘Here,’ he said, ‘put this on.’

‘Thank you.’ Sophie slid her arms into the robe and stared at him doubtfully from the sanctuary of her pillows. ‘You’re a doctor?’ she said. It didn’t really come as that much of a surprise to her. After all, the bride and groom worked in a hospital, and so a good many of their guests were likely to be medical professionals.

She was a doctor herself, a paediatrician at a hospital in the Cotswolds, but she didn’t want to share that information with him right now. This whole situation was way too embarrassing and she just wanted to escape from it as soon as she could. 'If that's the case, maybe you've managed to come up with a diagnosis of sorts?' Perhaps her tone was sharper than she intended. She was frazzled, and annoyed because she had found herself in this predicament.

He might well have detected her note of cynicism, but he made a show of taking her words at face value. 'Well, your pulse was racing,' he answered, 'and I suspect your blood pressure was sky high for a while. It occurred to me that you might be anaemic. If you're not eating properly, you might not be getting all the right nutrients—and, of course, being a woman, you'll be more prone to anaemia…'

'Yes,' she cut in swiftly. 'I don't believe you need to go into detail.' She frowned. 'And I doubt I'm anaemic. I'm just stressed, that's all. I've been stressed for weeks, with one thing and another.' She clamped her mouth shut. Why was she telling him her problems? How did she know if he was to be trusted?

'Not just because of Nathan, then?' His voice was soothing, coaxing her to divulge more.

She shrugged lightly, a movement that caused

the robe to slip, allowing a glimpse of bare shoulders. His gaze followed the movement, lingering momentarily on the creamy slopes until she tugged the robe back in place.

'I doubt he's really worth all that anxiety,' he murmured. 'You seemed quite keen to be free of him earlier. Perhaps you're at war with yourself.'

She shook her head. 'No, you're right, it isn't just that.' The end of a relationship was a bad thing, but she would get over it, wouldn't she? In fact she was already over it. Or at least, so she had thought, until Nathan had turned up here today. She gave a heavy sigh. 'I lost my parents a couple of months ago,' she explained. 'It was a shock. It was so unexpected. An accident.'

'I'm sorry.' He moved closer to her, laying a hand on her arm. 'That must have been dreadful for you…an awful tragedy.' He stroked her arm lightly, a gentle caress, like a breath of warm air gliding over her. It was meant to be a gesture of sympathy, to show her that she wasn't alone, but his touch seared her flesh and Sophie had to take a deep breath in order to calm herself and enable her to go on.

'It's not something you think will ever happen.'

'No. I don't suppose it is.' He lifted his hand to her face to smooth back the strands of hair that had fallen over her cheek. 'Do you have any brothers or sisters that can help you through this?'

She shook her head. 'There's no one…no family.' She hesitated, aware of his fingers following the line of her cheekbone, tucking the wayward tendrils of hair behind her ear. It was a strangely hypnotic motion that made her want to lean back into his embrace. It encouraged her to go on talking, to tell him everything that was going wrong with her life.

'So how are you coping? Not well, by the sound of things.'

'No—it's difficult, you see, because now I have to take over the running of the farm. I used to help out, but finding myself in charge has been a bit overwhelming.'

'I imagine it would be easier said than done.' He sounded curious.

She nodded. 'I'm at my wits' end, really. I have to keep going because if I don't do it, who else will see to the animals?' She thought about it, and about Nathan's reaction. 'I'd hoped Nathan might want to help out, him being a vet and all, but it seemed he had other things on his mind.'

She'd expected Nathan to understand what she was going through and to be supportive, but he had seemed preoccupied, and she had been left to muddle through on her own. She felt as though he had let her down when she needed him most.

'What sort of things?'

'Well, after my parents died, I inherited the farm, as well as money tied up in shares and investment bonds. Nathan was full of plans for what we might do with it.'

'You think the money was important to him?'

'I don't think it was the money in itself. I think it was just that it made him ambitious. He started to make plans, and he would talk about starting up a veterinary practice of his own—he'd need a large property and acres of land, he said, and he thought my farm, Woodvale, would be the ideal place for that. That wasn't what I wanted. I didn't want the house turning into business premises… it was my home.'

She frowned. 'I suppose I began to see him in a different light—he had started to take over, bit by bit. He was even planning Christmas without taking time to consider what I might want. We would go to Switzerland and spend the Christmas break in a ski lodge, he said, but I couldn't get my head around it. I'd always spent Christmas at home, with my parents and relatives. It seemed too much of a jump from that to going skiing, for me, at least. I began to feel as though I didn't know him at all.' She gave a short laugh. 'And yet the truth is, if I'd been sure of his love, I would have done anything for him. But somewhere along the way, he forgot to show me that he cared.'

'You thought your relationship had lost its way?'

'Yes. We'd been drifting apart for some time.' She frowned, thinking about it. It hadn't helped that she'd been ill. She'd been under par for some time, and perhaps she'd been working too hard, taking on too much, but, whatever the reason, her health had taken a battering these last few months. Her whole body seemed to ache, and she was constantly tired, and that was another thing that Nathan had found difficult to handle. Eventually, she'd gone to see her GP. So far, he hadn't been able to pin it down to anything specific, but he was doing tests.

In the meantime, Nathan had imagined she could simply pull herself together and shake it off, and she'd tried, she'd done her best to get on top of it, feeling guilty for not pulling her weight in the relationship. In the end, as the illness had lingered, it had finished things off between them, and she was left wondering if perhaps she would never experience true love and marriage. There was something wrong with her, and maybe she couldn't expect anyone to want her.

She looked up at Lucas. His expression was sombre, concerned, and she gave a ragged sigh. 'I don't know why I'm telling you any of this.'

'I think perhaps you needed to get it off your chest. It sounds as though this has been building up inside you for a long time, until it became too much for you, and perhaps that's why you fainted.' He drew her hand into his, holding it between his palms as though to show her he cared.

It felt so natural, that small, intimate gesture. She'd never met him until this evening, but it was as though he knew exactly what she needed. He was offering her comfort and compassion…those things that had been sorely missing from her life of late. But instinct warned her that she shouldn't read anything into it. She couldn't place her trust in anyone. Not any more.

'Perhaps I can help in some way,' he said softly. 'Even if you just need someone to talk to.'

She pulled in a quick breath. His offer filled her with temptation, but it wasn't to be, was it? 'Ah…there's the rub…you and I aren't likely to meet up again, are we? We're just strangers passing through.'

'It doesn't have to be that way,' he said. 'I'd like to see you again, just to know how you're getting along.'

He wasn't suggesting that he felt anything more than friendly concern, but she was on her guard, all the same. She had been burned once, and she'd learned her lesson. Besides, she had way too much on her plate right now for her to even think about getting involved with anyone.

She straightened up. 'I'm all right now,' she murmured. 'I ought to get dressed. Where did you put my frock?'

He frowned. 'Are you sure about that?' he asked. 'Perhaps you ought to rest a little longer.'

'I need to put in an appearance downstairs,' she said. 'My friends will be wondering what's happened to me.'

His gaze wandered over her, but he must have realised that she meant what she said, because he got to his feet and strode across the room. A moment later he came back with her dress, and handed it to her.

'Thank you,' she said. She took the dress from him and held it in front of her. 'If you don't mind...?'

'Of course.' He hesitated, reaching into his jacket pocket. 'I'll give you my number,' he murmured. 'That way, if you need me, you can give me a call.'

She glanced at the number he'd scrawled on the hotel stationery.

'Thanks,' she murmured. 'But, as I said, I'll

be fine.' She lifted her chin. 'Goodbye, Lucas. Thanks for your help.'

He sighed, then turned away from her and walked towards the door. 'I don't like goodbyes,' he said, halting momentarily to give her a fleeting glance before walking out into the corridor. There was a glimmer of something in his eyes, something that Sophie couldn't interpret.

The door closed behind him, and she sat for a while staring at the place where he had stood just a moment ago.

She had done the right thing, letting him go, hadn't she? He was interested in her, that was for sure, but she was in no state to get entangled with anyone else. Her life was a mess, and right now she didn't know whether she was coming or going.

Why, then, did it feel as though she'd just passed over something special?

CHAPTER TWO

'COME on, ladies,' Sophie called to the hens. 'Feeding time.' She scattered a mix of corn and pellets over the rough ground and immediately found herself surrounded by a huddle of excited, squawking poultry. Ferdie, the goose, preened himself, then thrust out his chest and paraded around the compound as if he owned the place, until it dawned on him that he was missing out because the hens were already busy tucking in.

Sophie threw down the rest of the feed and walked over to the gate. Suddenly, she felt a nudge from behind and was pushed forward against the fence, so that she had to put out a hand to steady herself.

'Don't do that, George,' she said crossly, turning to reprimand the goat. 'I've told you before, you mustn't butt people. It isn't polite. Wait your turn, and I'll feed you, too.' But George was taking no notice at all and nudged her again. She sighed. 'Why can't you be nice and placid like your mate, Jessie?' she queried. 'Look at her, she's munching grass. She's quite contented and she never gives me any trouble. Unlike you.' It occurred to her, though, that Jessie was maybe a little too content with life on the farm. She was always eating and she seemed to be putting on quite a bit of weight.

Still, she didn't have time to dwell too much on the animals' welfare just now. She was running late. Her shift at the hospital started in around three quarters of an hour and she still had to top up the ponies' hay and fill up the water troughs.

It was some twenty minutes later that she was finally ready to set off for the hospital. Glancing back at the lovely, stone-built farmhouse, where a late flush of roses clambered over the walls and mingled with lush, green ivy, she felt the familiar pang of loss as she drove away. It was a beautiful house, lovingly cherished by her parents, and she missed them dreadfully. This had been her home from as far back as she could remember, a place where she had always felt safe and secure, but now everything had changed. Her life had been turned upside down overnight after that fatal traffic accident.

Once she arrived at work, there was no time to settle into the day. 'You're wanted down in A and E,' the duty nurse told her. 'It's a five-year-old with breathing difficulties. He was brought in by ambulance a few minutes ago, and the registrar's asking for a paediatric consultation.'

'Thanks, Hannah,' Sophie said. 'I'll go down there right away. Is everything else going smoothly here?'

Hannah nodded. 'I'm doing observations on the children who were admitted overnight. There aren't any problems that I can see, so far, except that the boy with the congenital heart condition is still very weak. He's probably going to need surgery before too long, according to Mr Burnley.'

'I'll look in on him as soon as I get back.' Sophie shrugged into her white linen coat and took a stethoscope from her pocket before hurrying towards the lift.

'The registrar called for me to look at the young

boy with breathing problems?' she said to the house officer when she arrived in Accident and Emergency a couple of minutes later.

'That's right.' Debbie Logan, a pretty, newly qualified doctor with long, chestnut-coloured hair and grey eyes, led her to the treatment room where the little boy was lying in bed propped up by pillows. He was pale, and in obvious distress, with his breathing shallow and rapid. He was already attached to monitors that registered his pulse and respiratory rate and showed the activity of his heart.

'His blood oxygen level is very low,' Sophie commented. The child was being given oxygen through a face mask, but clearly it was Sophie's job to find out what was causing his difficulties.

She greeted the child's parents, who were sitting beside his bed looking extremely anxious. 'Hello,' she said. 'I'm Sophie Welland, the paediatrician. I understand that James was taken ill suddenly?'

'He's had a cough these last few days, and a bit of a wheeze,' his mother said. 'But it got worse in the early hours of this morning, and we were worried, so we called for an ambulance and he was brought straight to A and E.'

Sophie nodded. 'I'll listen to his chest, and we'll do some blood tests and get an X-ray, so that we can see what's going on.'

'That's what the other doctor said,' Mrs Coleman told her. 'He's already ordered tests, but he was called away to another emergency. He said you'd be down to look at James.'

Sophie looked over the boy's chart. The registrar had been thorough. The child had already been given antibiotics, and the doctor had ordered a nebuliser that would help widen the boy's airways.

'Ah, there you are. That was quick. I didn't expect you to get here quite so fast.' A strangely familiar male voice reached Sophie from across the room as she bent her head to carefully examine James a minute or so later. 'I thought we should admit him, but I wanted your opinion as to whether we should put in an airway. I'd say he was a borderline case, but I'll leave it to your judgement.'

Sophie withdrew the stethoscope from her ears

and let the instrument dangle from around her neck. She turned to see who was speaking, and immediately the breath caught in her lungs and all at once her throat was unexpectedly tight.

'Lucas,' she said, her blue eyes widening. A prickle of awareness ran down the length of her spine. He was the devil incarnate, as fiendishly good-looking as ever, with glittering grey eyes that held her fast and that right now were registering every bit as much surprise as her own. 'I didn't realise— I mean, I hadn't expected to see you here,' she added under her breath.

Her voice must have had a salutary effect on him, because he seemed to snap out of his stunned reverie and his mouth curved faintly in acknowledgement. 'That goes for me, too, Sophie,' he responded huskily, keeping his voice low, as though he was all too aware of the boy's parents close by. Not that they were paying any attention. They were watching the monitors and talking anxiously to one another.

'I'd hoped I might see you again,' Lucas said, 'but I must admit I hadn't expected it to happen quite so soon. Your friends were reluctant to give out your details, but all the same I felt sure I was pretty close to finding out where you lived.' His gaze moved over her. 'Somehow, I haven't been able to get you out of my mind since the wedding.'

Her cheeks flushed with hot colour. No wonder he had given her that odd look when he'd left her hotel room the other day. He'd never intended to give up on trying to find her, had he? She wasn't sure how she felt about that.

His shrewd smile told her he knew full well how he managed to get under her skin. Images of their last meeting filled her vision, causing a tide of heat to rush from her head to her toes and back up again. It was bad enough that he'd seen her half-naked, without adding to it that she'd given him her life history, and confided in him her worries about Nathan and the farm. She had always kept her private life to herself, but he had learned more about her in half an hour than anyone here had discovered in two years.

'I'd no idea that you were a doctor,' he said. 'It's great news to discover that we'll be working together.'

Sophie winced. From her standpoint it didn't bode well. 'But I've worked at this hospital for some time,' she said with a frown. 'How is it that I haven't seen you here before this?'

He gave a light shrug. 'I only started working here last week. I was brought in to take over from Dr Friedman when he left for the States.'

'Oh, I see.' She was struggling to come to terms with the fact that he was going to be her colleague from now on. How would her credibility as a doctor hold up with him knowing that she was harassed and finding it difficult to cope? And it was especially galling that he knew that lately she had been prone to dizzy spells.

She pulled in a deep breath and turned her mind back to their patient. 'I think we'll postpone the intubation for a while,' she said, doing her best to keep her manner professional. 'James is still conscious and coping, albeit none too well, without an airway, but it could be a traumatic procedure for him, and one that I'd sooner avoid if possible. I think we should add steroids to his medication...and check the levels of potassium in his blood. If they're too low, that could be adding to his problems. And of course we should admit him right away.'

'My thoughts exactly,' Lucas acknowledged. He gave a wry smile as though he knew just what was going on in her head. For her own part, she wanted to avoid even thinking about that night, but it stubbornly refused to go away. It stuck to her like a burr and irritated her just as much.

Lucas spoke to the child's parents, while Sophie managed to escape the room by going off to make arrangements for James to be admitted to Paediatrics. She was saddened to see the little boy looking so ill. He was frail, not speaking, too wretched to do anything but lie there.

She added her notes to his chart and went in search of the young house officer. She found her a few minutes later, by the reception desk, chatting with Lucas. Debbie was clearly taken with him, and who could blame her? The man oozed charisma and from the whispering she'd heard amongst the nurses in the last few minutes, Sophie guessed the new registrar had scored a direct hit with all the female staff. She stiffened. Men were capricious at the best of times when it came to lapping up the attention of young women, and it seemed that Dr Lucas Blake was no exception. All the more reason for her to steer clear of him!

She left the boy's chart with Debbie and started to head back towards Paediatrics.

Lucas caught up with her in the main corridor outside the treatment rooms. 'Sophie, wait…' He blocked her path, causing her to slow down and frown at him.

'I'm in rather a hurry,' she warned him. 'I have to go and see to my patients.'

'I understand… I know how busy you must be.' He smiled, looking her over, taking in the sleek lines of the figure-hugging dress she wore beneath her white coat. 'How is it that you always manage to look so good? Even a doctor's jacket looks great on you.'

Her gaze locked with his. 'I wouldn't waste your time trying to sweet-talk me, if I were you,' she told him. 'Other men have been down that road and, I promise you, I'm immune.'

He shook his head. 'So distrustful,' he murmured. 'Those men have a lot to answer for.' He studied her. 'I'm sorry if I took you by surprise back there—I was hoping we might meet under different circumstances. I'd planned on wining and dining you, and perhaps winning you round with soft lights and music.'

Her eyes narrowed on him. 'It sounds as though you were very sure of yourself.'

'Not exactly…but I wasn't about to give up on seeing you again.' He smiled. 'I'd do anything to see you relax and lose that worried look. It can't be right for you to be wound up quite so tightly.'

She pulled a face. He was probably right about her being wound up. Even now, she was stressed out. Her stomach was knotted, and there was a pain deep in her abdomen. Come to think of it, her hands ached, too. Weren't those all the signs of burnout? She was too young, surely? She was still a good two years off thirty. Perhaps she ought to go back to her GP, to find out if there was any news on the tests he'd done.

'Problems?' He was watching her, studying her features, as though he would learn everything there was to know about her.

She straightened her shoulders. 'None at all.'

'Really? You know, the only time I've seen you looking truly serene was when you were stretched out on the bed, back at the hotel, oblivious to everything. You were exquisite, and oddly vulnerable, and I had the strangest urge to protect you from whatever it was that was haunting you.'

Sophie's composure began to falter. 'On balance,' she managed, 'I dare say we should forget all about what happened the other day. I'd far sooner put it behind us.'

'Of course.' A faint smile played over his beautifully moulded mouth, and Sophie felt her stomach tighten all over again. He might as well have taken a photograph—she knew, and he knew, that her image was printed on his brain for evermore.

She stiffened her shoulders. 'I really need to get back to Paediatrics, Lucas. I have to see a young patient with heart problems, and I want to be there when James arrives on the ward.'

He nodded. 'Maybe we could meet up at lunchtime? I'd love to hear how you're getting on at the farm. My parents are in the same line of business, so if you have any worries on that score, I might be able to help.'

'I'm sure I'll manage—unless…' she gave a crooked smile '…you have any ideas on how to curb a playful goat who won't stop butting people at inopportune moments? His horns are curved, but they can be quite tough, and I can tell you I'm getting quite sore.'

He laughed. 'No wonder you're feeling the strain. I'd be the same way if I had to fend off an aggressive goat before work. A bit of padding down your jeans, perhaps? All I know is, it's best to train them off the habit when they're young.'

She nodded. 'Yes, we tried that, but George is very stubborn. He thinks he rules the roost—along with the goose, who believes it's his job to keep the hens in order.' She glanced at her watch. 'Sorry, but I must go.'

'I'll see you at lunchtime, then? One o'clock, in the restaurant. My treat.'

'Maybe,' she said. 'If I can get away.' With any luck, she'd find a reason why she needed to be on the ward at one o'clock. Instinct warned her that she should steer clear of Lucas. He was keen to start up some kind of relationship with her, and that was the last thing she wanted. She'd been hurt before, and she wasn't looking to go that way again.

He watched her walk away, and she felt his gaze scorching into her back as she went through the wide glass doors and out into the corridor. He was persistent, that was for sure.

On the paediatric ward, Sophie went to see Marcus, her little patient who was suffering from heart problems. He was four years old, a generally bright, happy child, but he was back in hospital right now, suffering from shortness of breath and trouble with his blood pressure. He was receiving oxygen through tubing that fitted into his nostrils.

'Hello, Marcus,' she greeted him. He had dark, tousled hair, and mischievous brown eyes that sought her out whenever she was close by. Now he was concentrating hard on a jigsaw puzzle, his tongue thrust out over his lower lip as he searched for the right piece. 'How are you getting on with the puzzle?'

Marcus frowned. 'Can't find pussycat's ear,' he said. 'I had it, but then my leg hurt and jumped up and it made me knock the puzzle over. It went…

whoosh.' He waved his arms in a wide arc to show Sophie what had happened.

'Oh dear…so now you've had to start all over again?'

He nodded.

'That's a shame…but you seem to be doing very well, all the same. You've done half of it already.'

It was worrying that he'd started having leg cramps again—it was a sign that the circulation to the lower half of his body was weak, one of the symptoms of his condition. He had been born with a narrowing of the aorta, the main blood vessel of the heart, and that could only be corrected by surgery.

She looked around. 'I wonder if any of the puzzle pieces fell on to the floor?' Bending down, she searched the area around his bed, and came up triumphantly a moment later with two pieces of puzzle. 'Aha…I think we've found the kitten's ear,' she said with a smile, handing them over. 'Perhaps you could put them in place, and then I'll check your blood pressure?'

He nodded obligingly. He was a good-natured

boy, and it tore at Sophie's heart that his body let him down.

She left him at work on his puzzle a few minutes later, and went to speak to the nurse. 'I'm going to alter his medication,' she told Hannah as she wrote instructions on his chart. 'We'll give him a slightly higher dose to strengthen the contractions of the heart. That should help ease the leg cramps. Did Mr Burnley say when he was hoping to operate?'

Hannah shook her head. 'He's talking to the parents now. He wants to do an echocardiogram so that he can see how the heart is working. He's scheduled it for tomorrow morning.'

'Good.' It was a simple, non-invasive procedure, using ultrasound to transfer images of the heart in action on to a computer screen, and it wasn't something that would upset Marcus in any way. 'Let's hope the medication does the trick. The sooner we can get him stabilised, the sooner he can have surgery.'

Sophie spent the rest of the morning tending to the other patients on the ward. One o'clock came and went, and it was only when Lucas startled her by coming onto the ward that she remembered she was supposed to have met up with him. Seeing him stride briskly into her territory filled her with unease. What would it take for him to realise that she really didn't want to get to know him better?

'Since you didn't come to the restaurant for lunch,' he remarked, walking to where she stood by the nurses' station, writing up her notes, 'I thought I'd better bring lunch to you.'

He was holding two sturdy, waxed carrier bags, and she frowned, wondering what on earth he had brought with him. 'Um…we've been really busy here this morning,' she murmured.

'Of course. It's like that down in A and E all the time. The only difference is we encourage staff to take their breaks whenever possible, otherwise they'll begin to flag before the day is out.'

He glanced around the ward. 'Everything looks fairly peaceful here at the moment. Dare I hope that you might come and share some food with me?' He lifted a dark brow in invitation, wafting one of the bags in front of her nose. A delicious aroma of cinnamon, fruit and pastries filled the air, and in spite of herself Sophie's mouth began to water.

'I take it you haven't already eaten?' he queried.

She shook her head. 'Not since I grabbed a cereal bar this morning. I should have stopped for a snack midmorning, but you know how it is—something cropped up.'

He tut-tutted. 'It won't do, you know. Doctors have to take care of themselves. How else can they expect to be fit enough to take care of their patients?' He looked around. 'Is there somewhere we can go to sit and eat this?'

She frowned. It would be criminal to let that food go to waste. 'The office is empty right now,' she suggested. 'There's a kettle in there, so we can have a hot drink if you like.'

'No need,' he said, 'unless you'd rather have tea. It's all in hand. I brought coffee along with me.'

'Okay.' She showed him into the office, and then peered into the carrier bags that he set down on the desk. 'Goodness! You thought of everything.'

His grey eyes crinkled. 'I do my best.' He began

to take out packages, and Sophie watched as appetising dishes appeared one by one.

'I'm overwhelmed.' Sophie smiled as she surveyed the feast. 'It's everything I might have bought for myself.'

'It just goes to show that great minds think alike,' he murmured, setting out cutlery on the desktop. He sat down opposite her. 'So, how come you only managed a cereal bar this morning? If that's how you normally go on, it's no wonder you have fainting attacks.'

'Like I said, I'd really rather forget about that,' she answered, frowning. 'I told you I was stressed. It's just that there's so much to do, what with feeding the animals twice a day and making sure they're clean and comfortable. Then there are the eggs to collect, and the fruit needs picking before it rots on the stems. We grow several different kinds of fruit on the farm—strawberries, raspberries, redcurrants and cranberries.'

She drew in a quick breath. 'It's late in the season, but a good many of the plants are still fruiting because they're under cover in polythene tunnels. I should have started on it before this, but there's been so much to do. It was okay when my parents were alive, because they took care of everything. I helped out when I could, but coping with all this on my own is a bit beyond me at the moment.'

Her expression was thoughtful. 'The cranberries, especially, are ripe for picking. Every year I would help my mother gather them in, and then we would make cranberry sauce, jar upon jar of the stuff, ready for the Christmas season. She'd give it away to friends, neighbours, anyone who wanted it, really.' She picked up her fork. 'I don't know what I'll do this year. It won't seem the same somehow. Christmas is going to be nothing like what it was before. How could it be?'

'The first year will be the worst.' He frowned. 'I'm sure your friends will be keen to invite you to their places, though. After all, it's a time when you should be with other people.'

'Maybe. Or I could go and help out at a refuge, or somewhere.'

'You have a while yet to think it through.' He sprinkled cheese over his baked potato and dug in a fork. 'In the meantime, maybe you should think of bringing in some help around the farm.'

She nodded, causing her honey-blonde hair to glide silkily over her shoulders. 'I thought of asking around in the village. I put an advert in the local paper, but so far no one's answered. There might be some teenagers looking for part-time work, though. I suppose I could put a notice in the newsagent's shop. I already have people to help with the other crops—we grow vegetables and corn, but they aren't really a problem. It's just the animals that I worry about.' She helped herself to salad, enjoying the crisp flavours and the sweet tang of mayonnaise.

She glanced at him. 'You said that your parents have a farm. I suppose you must have been brought up there?'

'Not exactly. It's something they took up after they opted for early retirement, but they've taken to it surprisingly well. I suppose it's what prompted me to move to the area. My sister and her family came over here to be near them, and I decided to follow suit. We've always been close as a family, and this part of the Cotswolds appealed to me—it's really lovely. I worked at one of the hospitals in the surrounding area for a time, and then this post came up, exactly what I wanted, so I grabbed it with both hands.' He swallowed a mouthful of coffee. 'As to the farm, it's more the kind of place where people can visit—children come to see the animals or play in the hay barn. And then there are trailer rides and a play area.'

Her mouth curved. 'It sounds wonderful. What did your parents do before they retired?'

He added salad to his plate. 'My father was a GP and my mother worked as a health visitor. Even my sister, Ella, joined the profession. She was a nurse, but she gave it up when she and her husband started a family.' He grinned. 'It's something she seems to be good at—she's pregnant again. This will be her third child.'

Sophie thought about that for a moment. 'I think it would have been good to be part of a family like that. I was an only child, but I often wished I had a brother or a sister.' She lifted her shoulders briefly. 'It wasn't to be.'

'It happens that way, sometimes. I was fortunate.' He helped himself to a spiced fruit bun. 'So how did you come to study medicine?'

She took a sip of coffee before she answered him. 'I'm not sure when it began, but I've always known that I wanted to work with children. Perhaps it was because I had no brothers and sisters. I was around eleven years old when our neighbours' children were taken ill with meningitis, and that had a profound effect on me. They were my friends and I was scared they might not get better, but our GP rushed them into hospital and when they came home a few weeks later, they were fine. I was impressed. I thought hospital work was something I might do later on.'

'I think you chose the right career. You were very good with James earlier—tender, caring and professional at the same time. His parents are reassured that he's in good hands.'

'I'm glad they feel that way.' She finished off her coffee. 'He settled into the ward well enough, and he's sleeping now, which is probably a good thing. I doubt he had much rest last night with all his breathing difficulties.'

He nodded, and then gave her a musing glance. 'Does it ever bother you, working with children?'

'Oh, yes.' It was a heartfelt statement. 'All the time. I'd defy anyone to be blasé about it. But it's rewarding, too.' She thought about young Marcus, with his engaging smile, and brightened. 'Children take life as it comes and grab it with both hands. It's lovely to see what a wonderland it is for them. Everything is new and exciting, and sometimes it's refreshing to look at the world through their eyes.'

His gaze trailed over her. 'I'm sure they love having you as their doctor.'

'I hope so. I do my best.' She wiped her hands on a serviette and surveyed the remains of their lunch. 'We seem to have polished that off between us with no trouble at all. Thank you for that,' she said, returning his gaze with real appreciation.

It was hard to imagine why he was going to so much trouble to feed her and get to know her, but it would have been churlish of her not to acknowledge his efforts. Perhaps he was more concerned about her fainting on him than she had realised, and that was the real reason he was keeping an eye on her.

There was a knock on the door, and Hannah looked into the room. 'Sorry to interrupt,' she said, 'but Mr Burnley's looking for you, Sophie. He wants a word with you before he goes off on his rounds.'

'Thanks, Hannah.' Sophie stood up. 'I'll go and find him.' She glanced at Lucas. 'I'm sorry to cut this short,' she said, 'but Mr Burnley's our cardiac surgeon, and I wouldn't want to keep him waiting.'

'That's all right, I understand.' Lucas began to clear away the remains of their feast. 'I'll take the opportunity to go and look in on young James while I'm here, if I may.' He gave the nurse a look that would have set fire to steel. 'Perhaps Hannah would show me where he is?'

Flustered, Hannah stared at him, her mouth dropping open a little. 'You want *me* to take you to him? Um…yes…yes, of course. I can do that.' She pulled herself together, as though she realised she was babbling. 'I was forgetting you're new around here. He's in the bay along the corridor. If you want to follow me, I'll lead the way.'

'Thank you.' Lucas's smile had an even more devastating effect on Hannah's composure. He walked to the door, holding it open so that she could retreat into the corridor, and for just a second their fingers touched. Hannah looked as though her senses were in a whirl, and Sophie could see that she was trying desperately to get a hold on herself.

A wry smile edged Sophie's lips. It was just as well she'd made up her mind to steer clear of Lucas. He was obviously pure dynamite, and she'd no intention of becoming his next conquest.

CHAPTER THREE

'HOW is our little patient doing?' Lucas was frowning as he walked towards the bed in the paediatric bay of the emergency unit. It was some days later, and Sophie was getting used to seeing him about the place.

'Not so badly now,' Hannah said on a heartfelt sigh, 'but I can tell you, that was a worrying hour or so.' She glanced at Sophie. 'For a while there, I thought we were going to lose her.'

Sophie nodded. 'Me, too.' She stretched, easing the ache in her lower back. It was mid-afternoon and she had been working full out all day, first with her charges on the paediatric ward and now with this small child who had been rushed to hospital by ambulance.

'Her parents had no idea she would have such a bad reaction to nuts,' Lucas commented. 'They'll have to be extra careful from now on.' He gazed down at the small child, whose fair curls tumbled over the pillow. The five-year-old's face was drained of colour so that she was almost as pale as the sheets. 'Still, she seems to be a lot more comfortable now.'

'Yes, she does. It was lucky you managed to get in an airway before the swelling in her throat became too severe.' Sophie glanced at him. Her respect for Lucas had grown by leaps and bounds over the last hour or so. By all accounts, he had worked desperately to save this little girl before calling Sophie down for a consultation, and as soon as she had set foot in A and E she had been able to see for herself how capable he was, and how gentle and caring he had been with the child.

Hannah was right. It had been touch and go for a while, but after all Lucas's efforts and a further shot of adrenalin, the child was at last beginning to recover, to everyone's relief.

'She'll need to be observed over the next few hours,' Sophie said, dragging her thoughts away from Lucas to the job in hand, 'so we'll admit her to the paediatric ward.' She glanced at Hannah. 'We'll keep Sarah on IV fluids for a while, with the addition of a low-dose steroid and an antihistamine.'

'Okay, you can leave it with me.' Hannah went to check on the IV fluids, and Sophie went to find a computer in the doctors' writing-up area where she could sit down to type up her notes.

Lucas followed her, coming to sit on the edge of the desk, watching her as she worked and making her all too conscious of his powerful, overwhelmingly male body. She sent him an oblique glance, her fingers pausing on the keyboard. 'Have you made arrangements for the parents to talk with a specialist?' she asked him, trying to keep her voice on an even keel. He was long and lean, flat stomached, and just having him close by made her abdomen tighten and had all of her senses in a flurry.

He nodded. 'I told them I would make an appointment for Sarah to see an immunologist.'

'Good. Sometimes, if things are handled the right way, the allergy might disappear completely after a few years.'

'True. Let's hope she's one of the lucky ones.' He stayed silent while she finished inputting the data, and when she leaned back in her chair, arching her back and suppressing a faint yawn, his gaze trailed over her.

'How are things with you?' he murmured, a hint of concern coming into his eyes. 'You look tired. Are you still overdoing things?'

'It's good of you to ask, but I'm fine, thanks,' she answered, absently curling and uncurling her fingers to dissipate the ache in her knuckles. It wasn't the truth, but rumours spread like wildfire in this place, and she didn't want it broadcast that she was under the weather and feeling the strain. She had a responsible position to uphold, and the last thing she needed was for people to think she couldn't cope.

'Hmm.' It was clear he didn't believe her. 'You're very pale. Are you quite sure you aren't anaemic?'

'Like I said, I'm fine.' She was compounding the lie. She'd been so tired lately, that it was quite possible she *was* anaemic, but at least she'd done the responsible thing and paid another visit to her GP. He had found some problems with the haemoglobin levels in her blood, but wanted to know more about what was causing these, along with her other symptoms, and had ordered another set of blood tests. As soon as the results from those were back, hopefully she'd know if her problems were physical or simply the result of all the stress she'd been under of late. Not that she'd want Lucas to know any of that. All she actually wanted right now was to go and take her long overdue break. Perhaps a cup of coffee would perk her up a bit.

'You're very cagey, aren't you?' Lucas commented in an amused tone, as he tried to fathom her expression. 'I wonder if Nathan's responsible for that, or whether you've always been that way?'

'Perhaps it comes from being an only child,' she murmured, logging out of the computer. 'In some ways, it has its advantages. You learn to appreciate your independence.'

'And miss out on so much.' He studied her briefly. 'You make it hard for anyone to get close to you—or perhaps it's just me that you have a problem with.' He frowned. 'But that only makes me all the more intrigued.' He shook his head in a perplexed fashion. 'I'm not quite sure what it is about you that has me all fired up…but I can't help feeling that I need to shield you from whatever life is throwing at you. Maybe it's that we seem to be opposites—the fact that I have a strong family to back me up, while you appear to be all alone in the world and put up a defensive front—but whatever the reason, I definitely want to get to know you better, Sophie…and I'll do it, sooner or later.'

She shook her head. 'Like I said, you don't need to do that.'

His pager began to bleep, and he checked the text message before turning his attention back to her. 'Sorry Sophie, but I have to go,' he said, his brow creasing. 'Something about a pregnant woman with high blood pressure.'

'That doesn't sound too good.' She stood up, preparing to follow him into the main reception area.

'No, it doesn't.' He sent her a thoughtful look. 'Are you heading back to Paediatrics, or will you be able to find time to take a break? We do great coffee down here in A and E. And I keep a snacks table on hand for the staff. You could help yourself from it, and maybe go and sit in the garden room for a while. It might make you feel better.'

She gave him a wry smile. So much for her trying to fob him off. He hadn't believed a word she'd said, had he?

'I'm not sure… I was due a break over an hour ago.' The cafeteria was two flights up, and didn't hold out much appeal for her at the moment. She wanted sunshine and fresh air and a complete change of scenery. Perhaps that would help to lift her spirits.

'There are glazed fruit tarts…and jam doughnuts,' he said in a coaxing fashion as they walked towards the treatment area. 'And salad sandwiches, freshly made, with bread bought this morning from the bakery down the road…and cheese. You like cheese, don't you? It's very good for you—full of—'

She laughed. 'Enough,' she said. 'You don't need to go on. You've convinced me. I'll grab something from the snacks table and take it out into the garden room.' It would be good to enjoy the late October sunshine.

'Good.' He looked pleased with himself. 'I'll come and join you just as soon as I can…as soon as I've taken a look at this young woman.'

Sophie's brows rose a fraction. She might have known there was a hidden motive in his attempt to get her to stay around. What was it with Lucas that he wasn't prepared to give up on her? Was she some kind of a challenge to him? So far she seemed to be the only female in the hospital who didn't swoon at his mere presence! Or perhaps she presented him with a medical conundrum that he needed to solve?

The thought pulled her up sharply. Why would any man be drawn to a woman whose life was marred by illness? Hadn't she learned that lesson with Nathan? He might have attempted to start up the relationship with her again at the wedding, but that would have been a short-lived exercise. As soon as he realised she was still plagued by symptoms he would have dropped her like a hot brick. And eventually Lucas would do the same.

It would be better if she didn't think about it

any longer, though. Weren't there enough complications in her life without adding him to the list?

They parted company a few minutes later, and Sophie made her way to the sunlit garden room. She was alone in here, and for a while she enjoyed the solitude. The glass doors were open a little to let in a light breeze, and she could see white tables and chairs set out on the terrace beyond.

She chose a table by the door, and breathed in the fresh air. Yellow jasmine scrambled over trellised wooden panels, and here and there stone tubs were filled with autumn flowers, yellow and bronze chrysanthemums and bold, white asters with yellow centres. At intervals there were tall green palms that added a restful touch.

She sat down and began to eat from the selection of food on her tray. The fruit pie was cool and refreshing, and instead of coffee she had chosen fresh orange juice. It wasn't too long before she began to feel her batteries recharging. Maybe there was nothing wrong with her after all. The thought cheered her, and she looked around, happy with her surroundings, drawing energy from the complete break from work.

A short time later, she heard children's voices coming closer. A line edged its way into her brow. Did the youngsters belong to someone who worked here? This was a place where the staff could rest a while, so they weren't likely to be the offspring of patients.

'Is Mummy very poorly?' The voices came nearer, and Sophie looked around to see Lucas coming towards her, holding the hands of a fretful young girl, around six years old, and a little boy who looked to be a year or so younger.

'She needs to rest. That's why she's going to stay in hospital for a while, so that we can take good care of her.' Lucas's voice was warm and reassuring.

Sophie stood as he approached the table,

'Lucas, is anything wrong?' She could see from his grim expression that his return to the hub of A and E had turned out very differently from what he had expected.

He nodded. 'The patient I was paged for,' he answered quietly, 'turned out to be my sister Ella.

I didn't realise who she was until I went to see her because no one had her details.' He put an arm around each of the children's shoulders and drew them forward. 'These are my niece and nephew, Emily and William. Apparently they were out on a shopping trip together when Ella was taken ill.'

Sophie could only imagine what he was going through, but she kept up an appearance of calm, so as not to upset the children. 'Hello,' she said, smiling at them. 'I'm sorry to hear that your mother is poorly…but I know that your uncle will look after her very well. He's a very good doctor.'

William nodded. 'I know.' He was frowning, his grey eyes confused, and Sophie guessed he was trying his utmost to come to terms with what had happened.

'It must have been a shock for you,' she said, looking from one to the other. 'Do you want to tell me about it?'

William shook his head, but Emily couldn't contain herself and blurted out, 'Mummy fainted.

A lady in the shop had to help us. We didn't know what to do. We couldn't make Mummy wake up.'

Sophie wanted to put her arms round the little girl and give her a hug. 'You must have been very frightened.' William didn't give way to his emotions. He was still trying to be stoical, but surely it couldn't be good for him to keep everything bottled up inside?

She glanced at Luke. 'Was there any indication that this might happen? How was she in her previous pregnancies?'

'It was plain sailing with both Emily and William but she has found this third pregnancy much harder. Really, I should have expected something like this. She's been complaining of headaches and blurred vision, and I could see that there was some swelling in her hands and around her ankles. I told her to talk to her obstetrician as a matter of urgency and check with the midwife. She said she would, but it doesn't look as though she carried it through.'

'I suppose she was busy with the children,' Sophie said in a low voice. 'Women don't always get their priorities right when they're looking after a family.'

'I'm beginning to realise that now.' Lucas encouraged the children to sit down, and Sophie offered them orange juice and sandwiches from her tray. William accepted the sandwich but sat holding it, not attempting to eat, while Emily sipped at a glass of juice. Her cheeks were flushed, and streaked with tears that had escaped.

Sophie felt in her coat pocket for her small stock of badges. She gave them to children on the paediatric ward whenever they had been brave or needed cheering up. 'Perhaps you'd like to colour these in,' she suggested. 'There's a teddy bear with a spotted necktie, and a teddy bear with a flowery vest. Choose which ones you want. I think I've some coloured pencils in my other pocket.' She delved around and produced half a dozen small pencils. 'There you are. Just the thing.'

Both children carefully examined the badges and after a while began to colour.

'What are you going to do?' Sophie asked

quietly, turning towards Lucas, who came to sit down next to her.

'We'll admit Ella for observation. Her blood pressure was way above what it should be, so we'll start her on medication to bring that down, and we're going to try magnesium sulphate to stabilise things before we give her steroid injections.'

Sophie nodded approval. Steroids would help the baby's lungs to mature, while magnesium sulphate would prevent seizures, which could be dangerous for both mother and baby.

'How far on is she?'

'Thirty weeks. I'd prefer to stabilise her, if we can, so that the baby can go to full term.' He clamped his lips together briefly. 'Of course, we may have no choice but to do a Caesarean if things don't improve.'

Sophie sucked in a silent breath. The problem with high blood pressure in pregnancy was that it could lead to eclampsia, a condition that might prove fatal. She reached out to Lucas and laid a hand on his. 'I'm sure you'll do everything you can for her,' she said. 'No one could do better.'

She watched the children carefully colouring the badges. 'What will you do about the children? Is someone coming to collect them?'

He shook his head. 'That's a problem I have to sort out—her husband is working away at the moment. I've given him a ring to let him know what's happened, and he's going to drive back straight away. Even so it will take him a few hours to get here. In the meantime, I have to take care of them.'

'What about your parents? Wouldn't they be able to help out?'

'Any other time, yes, I'm sure they would, but they're on a cruise at the moment, somewhere in the Mediterranean. So it's down to me. I'll have to find some way to keep them amused until Tom gets back.' He frowned. 'To be honest, I don't really have a clue. There isn't anything for them at my place—it's a straightforward bachelor pad, and I imagine they'll be stir crazy after an hour.'

'How long will it be until you go off-duty? I expect our play therapist could keep them amused for half an hour or so.'

He brightened. 'Do you think she'd mind? It

wouldn't be for too long—I'm off in an hour.' His brows drew together. 'At least that will give me time to think of a plan of action.'

'I'm sure Amy will be glad to help out.' Sophie watched a variety of expressions cross his face. He was worried, clearly, about his sister, but he seemed uneasy about the prospect of looking after the children. It was hard to understand the reason for that, because she'd seen him with children in A and E, and there was no doubt that he was good with them. He was always very capable as a doctor, patient and kind, and ready to listen, but this was family, and perhaps because it was so important to him he was afraid of messing up.

'I'll be finishing my shift in an hour, too,' she said. 'Do you think they'd like to come over to the farm? I'm sure that between us we can manage to keep them occupied for a few hours.'

He sucked in a deep breath, and then leaned over and wrapped his arms around her in a bear hug. It made her feel unexpectedly warm and cherished, emotions she hadn't felt in quite a while. They confused her, making her want more.

'I could kiss you for that,' he said, and for a

moment she thought he was going to follow through on the thought. He looked into her eyes, his head bending towards her, but then he held back, becoming very still all at once. He looked at the children and she wondered if propriety had made him think twice. The breath left her body in a slow sigh. She didn't know whether she was disappointed or relieved.

'I should go back to the ward,' she said. 'Would you like me to take the children with me?'

He appeared to be struggling, momentarily, to get a hold on himself, but then he nodded. 'But perhaps I should come with you, just to see them settled in.'

That made sense. The children didn't know her, so why would they want to go with her? Once they were involved with the play materials, it would be a different matter.

'Okay.'

Fortunately, William and Emily were distracted for long enough by the toys and activities that the play therapist put their way so that Sophie was able to go about her work.

'They've been fine,' Amy told her when she

went to collect them at the end of her shift. 'There were a few worries about their mother, but they were willing enough to try out the construction toys and the playhouse.'

'Thanks, Amy. I don't know what we would have done without you.'

They went to meet Lucas in the car park. 'Follow me,' she said, 'and I'll show you the way to the farm.'

Once they left the town, she drove through beautiful countryside, rich with rolling hills and lush woodland, and interspersed with the distinctive Cotswold stone houses, mellow and golden in the late-afternoon sunshine.

The children were enthralled by the farmhouse. 'Do you live here all by yourself?' William asked.

'Yes, I do.' Her lungs felt tight as she said it. It hadn't always been that way, and she felt the loss keenly.

'It's lovely,' Emily said, gazing around at the mature trees and flowering shrubs. 'It's very big, isn't it?'

'That's true,' Sophie answered. 'There's a lot of land at the back, meadows and a small brook, and there are buildings for the animals, and so on. Come on into the house, and I'll show you around.'

Lucas was equally impressed. 'It looks as though a lot of love has gone into this house,' he murmured. 'What is it? Seventeenth century?'

She nodded. 'It's a Grade II listed building, so it's very special.'

'It is.' He looked at it again, taking in the impressive gables and the mullioned windows with their ornate wrought-iron fittings. 'I hope you have someone to help you with the upkeep of it.'

'I have someone to help with the building maintenance,' she said with a smile. 'Otherwise I would be tearing my hair out by now.'

She took them through to the kitchen, a large, homely room with broad oak beams and golden, oak-fronted cupboards. A large range cooker was set into a deep stone recess and gave out an inviting background warmth.

'I have a beef casserole that I can heat up for supper,' she said. 'I just need to prepare a few extra potatoes, and there should be enough to feed all of us. Does that sound all right?'

'It sounds more than all right,' Lucas said with a smile. 'I really didn't expect you to feed us.'

'It's no trouble. Perhaps William and Emily would like to look at the playroom while I get things started? Some of my old toys are still in there. I don't think my parents could bring themselves to throw them away.' She gave a crooked smile. 'I think they were hoping for grandchildren someday—but at least they didn't badger me about that. Perhaps it was just as well that they were prepared to be patient.' A moment of sadness crossed her face. Now they would never see that future laid out for her.

The playroom was on the ground floor, another oak-beamed room with an inglenook fireplace. There was no fire in the grate right now, and instead there was an ornamental screen decorated with summer flowers.

'Oh, wow! Look at that!' Emily's eyes grew large with wonder when she saw the huge doll's house that took up one corner of the room. 'Can I see it? Can I play with it?'

Sophie nodded. 'Yes, of course you can.

William, too, if you like. There's a set of Victorian bendy dolls inside.'

She could see that William was torn between wanting to play with the house and perhaps wondering if it wasn't too much of a girly thing to do, but then Lucas stepped forward, opening up the two doors that made up the front of the house.

'This is fantastic,' he said, and she guessed he was doing it for William's benefit, as much as for Emily's. 'Look at the drawing-room with the grand piano, and the kitchen—the kitchen is wonderful. There are lots of copper pans hanging from a shelf on the wall, and there's a broom in the corner for sweeping the floor. It almost makes me wish I was five or six years old again.'

William's face relaxed, and he went with Emily to peer inside. There were gasps of admiration, and Sophie glanced at Lucas, making a discreet thumbs-up sign. 'If you get tired of playing with the house,' she told the children, 'there's a box of toys against the wall on the other side of the room. If you need me, just shout. We'll be in the kitchen or somewhere near at hand.'

'Be careful,' Lucas warned the children. 'Don't break anything.'

They left the children and went back to the kitchen, where Sophie set about preparing supper with Lucas's help. She offered him coffee, and then a brief tour of the house.

'I'd like that,' he said. 'I can't imagine how many rooms there are in a place this size.'

'Quite a lot,' she said with a laugh. 'Perhaps it will be a whistle-stop tour.' She led the way. 'Maybe we should start with the living room.'

This was another large room, again with an oak-beamed ceiling and large stone fireplace. The walls were panelled with pale oak, and decorated at intervals with pictures and family portraits.

'Those must be your parents,' Lucas remarked, studying a framed photograph of the three of them taken on her graduation day. 'They look awfully proud.'

Sophie nodded and tried to smile, but she was overcome by a sudden swell of emotion that blocked her throat. It was still so hard to accept that they were gone for ever.

'We don't have to do the tour if it's too painful for you, Sophie.' Lucas insisted, seeing her distress.

Shaking her head and putting on a brave face, Sophie smiled.

'My parents were very proud of their home and loved welcoming guests. Of course I'll show you around.'

Lucas was the perfect guest as they toured the rest of the house, commenting warmly on her parents' great taste.

'My mother was a great collector of beautiful things,' Sophie agreed. 'I suppose you could say that it is something of a family tradition and I was always keen to add to her collection.'

Sophie ran her hand absently over a beautiful crystal punchbowl, which held pride of place on the dining-room sideboard, wincing as her finger grazed the damaged edge.

'This was something of a family heirloom. I had thought to have it restored for her this year, but now…' Her voice trailed away as she wiped away a tear that threatened to trickle down her cheek.

'It's very dear to me. There are so many memories—my father would bring it out every Christmas Eve, and we would drink a toast, and that would be the start of Christmas celebrations. We'd have friends round, and it wouldn't be long before everyone was in the party spirit.'

She gave a faint smile, reminiscing. 'My father had his own special recipe for the punch, lots of fruit juices, some cider, a dash of brandy, and he'd slice up fruit to decorate the top. It was delicious, but most of all it was a family tradition, something we looked forward to every year.'

Lucas gave her a hug. 'I'm so sorry you're having to go through all this, Sophie. I think you should still try and get this bowl fixed. It might make you feel better. Let's box it up, shall we, and I'll have a look into where you could take it to be mended.'

'Maybe.' Sophie smiled at Lucas. 'I'm sorry for burdening you with my woes, Lucas, I'm supposed to be helping you out today!'

'You've been a great help, believe me. I had no idea how I was going to keep Emily and William amused, but they seem to really love it here.'

'I'm thrilled. It's nice for me to see my toys getting played with again after so long. Why don't you join them while I put the finishing touches to supper?' Sophie suggested.

Some half an hour later she laid the table and served up the casserole. 'Did you let your brother-in-law know where you are?' she asked Lucas as the children came to sit at the table.

'I did. He said he would go straight over to the hospital to see Ella, if that was all right with me. I said it was.'

'It's only natural that he would want to go there first. I imagine she'll be all the better for seeing him, and for the enforced rest in hospital.' She glanced at the children. 'It can't be easy, bringing up two youngsters, with another one on the way.'

She handed around plates, and soon everyone was tucking in. William and Emily were obviously hungry, and she guessed the small snack they'd had at the hospital had been barely enough to stave off the pangs.

The rest of the evening passed in a blur of chatter and laughter and as she waved Lucas and the children goodbye, Sophie realised that she was feeling happier than she'd felt in weeks, all thanks to Lucas's support.

It was best not to get too carried away with that thought. She guessed that he would do the same for any friend or colleague in distress. She didn't want to rely on his help, though. She couldn't afford to lean on him, could she?

Life had dealt her a few blows but she had to learn to tough things out for herself, and she would do it, no matter what it took.

CHAPTER FOUR

'YOUNG James looks very different from the way he did a few days ago, doesn't he?' Amy, the play therapist, glanced at Sophie as they stood by the nurses' station on the children's ward.

James was cuddling a soft toy, a black and white puppy, as he lay back against his pillows, watching a cartoon on TV. Sophie's mouth curved into a smile. 'He certainly does,' she said. 'It's hard to imagine that yesterday he was too weak to be bothered with anything, but now he's improving rapidly. His breathing's a lot better. If he continues like this, we should be able to think about discharging him soon.'

'That's great news. His mother will be over the moon.'

'I'm sure she will.' Sophie wrote up the boy's medication on his chart and went in search of Hannah. The nurse was checking Marcus's blood pressure, but she looked up as Sophie approached.

'Are you off down to A and E?' she asked.

'I am. I just wanted to ask if you would check up on James for me. I'm going to put him on salbutamol to help widen his airways, but I want him to use a plastic spacer to begin with. It will be easier for him to manage than an inhaler. Would you show him how to use it, please?'

'Of course, no problem.'

'Thanks, Hannah. I'll be down in Emergency if you need me for anything.'

Sophie headed for the lift. Trips down to A and E were a regular part of her job, but over the last couple of weeks things had changed. By now she was getting quite used to seeing Lucas down there. Sometimes she even found herself looking for him and there would be a sharp twinge of disappointment if he wasn't there. As it was, she hadn't seen him for a day or so, because she'd had some time off and their shifts had not coincided. It was odd to realise how much she missed him.

This afternoon she found him in one of the

treatment rooms, working with Debbie Logan, the pretty, brunette house officer.

'Ah, there you are, Sophie,' he said, throwing her a quick look as she entered the room. He smiled, as though he was pleased to see her. 'We've another small patient for you here.' He bent his head once more, concentrating his attention on the toddler lying in the cot, and for a moment or two Sophie watched him at work. He was infinitely gentle, his whole demeanour centred on caring for the youngster. Her gaze drifted to his jet-black hair, cut short and beautifully styled, silky and inviting to the touch. 'She was brought in after she had a convulsion about an hour ago,' Lucas added in a low voice. 'She hadn't had one before, but she started convulsing again a couple of minutes ago.'

Sophie pulled herself together and moved forward to look more closely at the child.

She was about two years old, with flushed cheeks, her eyes rolling back in her head and her body making jerky movements. It was frightening to witness the infant thrashing about that way, but for the mother, who stood to one side of the bed, watching, it must have been far worse. The woman's face was anguished and Sophie felt her pain as if it were her own.

She looked around for the toddler's chart. 'Have you given her diazepam to control the seizure?'

Lucas nodded. 'I gave it to her just a couple of minutes ago, but it will probably take a while to act. She's had an antipyretic, too, but again we have to wait to see if it will bring the fever down.'

'We should do blood tests,' Lucas said, turning to Debbie. 'It could be that she's suffering from an infection of some kind, so we need to do a full blood count, ESR, U&E, coagulation, PCR, glucose and culture.'

Debbie nodded. 'I'll see to it.'

'We'd better get a urine sample as well.' Sophie gazed down at the toddler. The girl's hair was damp with perspiration. If ever she had a child, she would hate to see her going through something like this.

Lucas glanced at Debbie once more. 'This is your first stint with Paediatric Emergency, isn't it? How are you coping?' He kept his voice low, but it was unlikely the mother was paying any attention. She was watching her child the whole time.

Debbie's expression was uncertain, and she pushed back a glossy tendril of hair that had escaped from its clip. 'I'm all right with it, on the whole, but it's emotionally draining sometimes. I suppose I'd expected that, but the reality is somehow much worse.' She looked at Sophie. 'I don't know how you can work with children all the time and still keep cheerful. You always look so confident and capable.'

'Thank you for that,' Sophie said with a smile, 'but I think the children themselves show you the way to keep going. They're down one minute and up the next, and once they're feeling better, there's no holding them back. Seeing them recover makes everything worthwhile…for me, at any rate.'

Debbie shook her head. 'I have to do these six months in Paediatric Emergency as part of my training, but I'm not sure I could do the job full time. It must take a special kind of person to stick with it.'

Lucas was stroking the little girl's hair, easing

it away from her face. She was wearing just a vest and pants, in order to keep her as cool as possible, but there was a sheet at the end of the cot, ready to draw over her once her condition stabilised. Slowly, the fit came to an end, and the child opened her eyes. She looked dazed, confused and very sleepy.

'She's coming out of it, isn't she?' her mother asked.

Sophie nodded. 'She'll probably sleep for a while now, and when she wakes up, it's doubtful that she'll remember anything about it.'

'Will it happen again?'

Sophie hesitated, not wanting to add to the woman's stress. 'It's possible...but if we can bring her temperature down and find out what was causing the fever, she should soon start to recover. All the same, I think we should admit her for observation, and wait for the results of the tests.'

'All right. Thank you.' The mother went to the child's side and started to speak gently to her. Lucas stepped away, to give her more room, and went over to Sophie.

'Perhaps you could take the parents to one side and talk to them about seizures?' he suggested softly.

'I will. I'll take them to the relatives' lounge.'

'Thanks. Now that Chloe's out of the woods for the moment, I want to grab the chance to go and look in on my sister. She had a difficult night, apparently, and I want to check up on her.' He turned to Debbie. 'Do you think you'll manage down here for a while? It looks as though Chloe's fallen asleep now, but you can page me if there are any problems, and Dr Carlson will be on duty any minute now, so you could refer to him for help if the consultant's tied up.'

'I'll be fine,' Debbie said. 'Don't worry about me. You've been holding my hand for the last few weeks. It feels as though it's time for me to stand on my own two feet.'

He smiled and laid a hand lightly on her shoulders. 'You're doing very well,' he murmured. 'But if there's anything that bothers you—anything at all—you only have to come to me.'

Watching them, Sophie felt uncomfortably like an intruder. Lucas had a naturally helpful manner, and perhaps that's what drew women to him. He was a good listener and he offered a broad shoulder to lean on.

Hadn't she been leaning on him rather too much of late? He'd been there for her when she'd passed out, and he'd been there to cheer her up when she'd been overwhelmed by grief at her house. It could be that she might begin to rely on him too much, and that wouldn't do at all, would it?

She went over to the child's mother and invited her to go along with her to the relatives' lounge for a chat. 'Dr Logan will stay and take care of Chloe. She'll be safe with her, and she'll probably sleep for some time. It's quite usual for young children to do that after seizures. In the meantime, we could go and find your husband and get a cup of coffee and then I'll do my best to explain the situation to you and answer any questions you might have.'

'Okay, thanks.'

Sophie left the room with the woman, turning back to catch a glimpse of Lucas reaching out to lightly clasp Debbie's arm as she would have turned away. Perhaps he was only trying to get the junior doctor's attention but, whatever the reason, Sophie felt the clutch of something indefinable tightening her stomach.

She tried to push all thoughts of him out of her head. Instead, she spoke to the parents for some time, answering their questions until they were both a little easier in their minds about what was happening to their daughter. Then, after she had given them leaflets to read on febrile seizures, she left them to talk things over and made her way back to A and E.

'I'll make arrangements to transfer Chloe to Paediatrics,' she told Debbie. 'We'll need all her case notes, referral forms and so on.'

'I'll see to it.'

'Thanks.' She glanced at the junior doctor. 'I'm sure you'll get along fine with Lucas to help you. He seems to have a sure touch, with both adults and children.'

Debbie nodded. 'I'm beginning to see that,' she said. 'The only thing that seems to faze him is looking after his niece and nephew—he talked to me about it, and I know he feels obliged to take care of them. A problem has cropped up again today so he might need to watch over them for a few hours after work. I think he worries about how to keep them occupied.'

Sophie frowned. 'I thought Ella's husband, Tom, had come back home to take care of them?'

'He did, but after a couple of days he was called back for an important meeting. A crisis has developed at the company he works for—he has to sort out the situation when things go wrong, and apparently they've discovered dangerous microbes in the water system. As the manager, he has to take charge and deal with the situation before it becomes a hazard for the workers.'

'Oh, dear.' Sophie winced. 'That's not good timing, is it?' She straightened, getting ready to transfer the toddler to Paediatrics. It was good of Lucas to step in and take care of his niece and nephew. Clearly, he took his responsibilities seriously.

Sophie went back to the children's ward and made sure that Chloe settled in all right. 'We'll keep her under observation,' she told Hannah. 'Hopefully she'll have no more seizures and it will mean just a short stay for her in hospital.'

Just before the end of her shift, she was surprised when Lucas stopped by the ward. He paused to say hello to the children who were well enough to take notice, before homing in on Sophie.

'I hope you don't mind, but I'm here to ask a favour of you,' he said, leaning against the desk at the nurses' station and watching as she filled in request forms for the lab. 'Do you think I could bring the children to the farm after work today… if you'll be home? Would that put you out too much? Only they're very upset about Ella being in hospital, and I'd like to find something that will distract them for at least a couple of hours until my parents can take over.'

'Are your parents home from their holiday, then?'

He nodded. 'They arrived home this morning, but they need time to sort themselves out, and of course they want to go and visit Ella in hospital.'

'That's understandable. It must be a worrying time for all of you.'

'Yes, it is, but there are practical problems, too, with Tom having to shoot off back to work. The children seem to like it well enough at my house, but I'm sure they'd love to see the animals at your place...if it wouldn't be too much of an imposition?'

'Of course you can bring them. We didn't really get a chance to show them around outside last time, did we?'

He smiled. 'That's true, but I think they had a great time, all the same. They were talking about their visit the next day, so it certainly made an impression on them.' His gaze flicked over her, a thoughtful expression shaping his features. 'I've been worrying about you—in fact, I rang you a couple of times over the next couple of days, but you weren't answering your phone. I guessed you were either out or busy. Have you been feeling okay?'

She nodded. 'Yes, thanks. I'm sorry if I didn't answer your calls. I've been having a few problems with my phone's battery.'

She placed the last of the forms into the wire basket on the table, and checked that all her paperwork was complete. 'That's me finished for the day,' she murmured. 'Will you be following me home, or do you have to stay on here for a while?'

'I'm finishing soon. I just have to go and collect the children from Ella's ward, and then I'll bring them over to the farm.'

'That's great.' She looked into his eyes, pleased that he was going to be around for the next hour or so. It still felt strange going back to the big, old house. Living there, all alone, it seemed that the place was echoing and empty. It was all the more reason why she couldn't face spending the Christmas season alone there…a time when family and friends should be together.

She made an effort to shake off those thoughts, and asked, 'How is your sister getting on? Do you think she'll be in hospital for much longer?'

'They'll keep her in for at least another week, I gather. The nurse told me she was uncomfortable last night, but she's improving slowly. Her blood pressure's going down, and the baby seems to be progressing well enough, so we're keeping our fingers crossed.'

'I'm glad.' She retrieved her bag from under the

desk and walked with him to the lifts. 'You said the children are upset. How are they managing?'

'Not too well. It's difficult for them when they go to see her. They start to get clingy and when the time comes they don't want to leave, and of course that upsets Ella, in turn, and her blood pressure shoots up again.'

She sent him a sympathetic look. 'It's difficult. I see it sometimes in reverse on the children's ward. Although the parents are encouraged to stay with the children as much as they like, there are some occasions when they have to leave, and both the parents and children get upset.'

'I can imagine. But William and Emily will be all the better for coming to see you, I'm sure.'

'Let's hope so, anyway.'

Sophie left him a short time later at the entrance to A and E and made her way to the car park. He would be at least three quarters of an hour behind her, she estimated, so that would give her time to rustle up something for them all to eat. There was salad in the fridge, a honey roast gammon, eggs, cheese and the fresh bread that she had picked up from the bakery at lunchtime.

If they had soup for starters, that would provide warmth for a cool, late October evening, and it should all serve to keep the pangs of hunger at bay for a while.

William and Emily bounced into her kitchen as she was putting the finishing touches to the dining table. 'Hi, Sophie,' they chorused, and she smiled a greeting and invited them to wash their hands and then sit down, ready to eat.

'We've been to see Mummy,' Emily told her. 'She's bored in hospital, 'cos she has to lie in bed all day, so I gave her some magazines to read. Uncle Lucas bought them for her.'

'And I gave her some flowers—pretty pink ones,' William put in. 'I don't remember what they're called, but Mummy said they were beautiful.'

'I'm sure she loved seeing both of you, more than anything,' Sophie commented, pouring boiling water into the teapot and setting it aside to brew.

'It looks as though you've been busy,' Lucas remarked, his gaze wandering over the jars of bright red cranberry sauce that were lined up on the worktop. Each jar had a little gingham cloth around the top, tied with ribbon, looking every bit like a product of a country farmhouse kitchen. 'So you decided to make the cranberry sauce after all?'

She gave a light shrug. 'I had to do something with all that fruit. I couldn't bear to see it rot on the branches…and I had the sugar, ginger and cinnamon and orange juice all ready in the cupboard, so there was no reason not to get started. Though I don't know how I'm going to manage even a jar at Christmas, all by myself.' She was thoughtful for a moment. 'I suppose I could take a few jars to the refuge and the local hostels, so the people there can have it with their Christmas turkey. And, of course, you must take some for your parents, and for Ella.'

'I'm sure they'll love it, thanks.' He smiled. 'My mother always makes her own Christmas pudding around this time of year. The smell of spices fills the kitchen, and makes your mouth water.' The smile turned into a rueful grin. 'Mind you, you have to be careful not to break your teeth on the shiny twenty pence piece she puts in it—that's a family tradition. Whoever gets the coin has to make a wish.'

Sophie chuckled. 'We did that, too.'

She glanced at Lucas. 'It sounds as though the children enjoyed visiting their mother. Have you been to visit your sister every day since she was admitted?'

He nodded. 'It's easy enough when I'm in A and E…and I think she's glad of the company.' He smiled. 'She was asking after you. She thinks the farm sounds great. She loves visiting my parents' place, especially in the spring, when all the baby animals are being born. Ella always was a softie.'

He said it with affection, and it was obvious that he thought the world of his sister. A small pang of regret flowed through her. Siblings might bring with them a dose of pain and suffering from time to time, but they could also bring unconditional love and arouse strong, protective instincts. She hadn't experienced any of those things, and she felt that loss deeply.

They finished their meal quickly and headed outside, before the children became restless.

William and Emily raced off across the floodlit yard towards the enclosure and the hen house. 'I'll give you some grain to throw down for the hens,' Sophie said. 'Just sprinkle it over the ground and they'll come and peck it up.'

Five-year-old William eagerly dipped his fingers into the bucket she held out to him, and pulled out a fistful of grain. He threw it down and clapped his hands in glee as the hens came towards him in a flurry of feathers.

Emily was more hesitant, gingerly casting the seed over the earth and drawing back as the hens approached her feet. 'Don't worry if they poke around your shoes,' Sophie told her. 'They're just curious. They won't hurt you. It's George, the goat, you have to watch out for. He thinks he owns the place, and he likes to nudge you out of the way if he gets the chance.'

Lucas chuckled and looked around. 'That's not likely to happen today. It looks as though you have him taken care of, for the time being anyway.'

Sophie nodded. 'I decided to tether him to an iron post, just while the children are here. He's on a long leash and he seems happy enough, so I'm sure he'll be fine.'

William had used up all the grain by now and was ready for more action. 'Can we go and see the ponies?' he asked, looking towards the paddock.

'Yes, of course.' Sophie hunted in the pockets of her jacket and produced a couple of small carrots. 'Here, hold onto these,' she said, giving the children one each.

Emily was puzzled. 'I don't eat carrots like this,' she said in a small voice. 'Mummy always cooks them first, and I have them with my dinner.'

Sophie laughed. 'They're for the ponies,' she explained. 'It will help you to get to know them if you give them a treat. Don't worry, I'll show you how to feed them.'

'Oh.' Emily looked relieved, and Lucas laid a reassuring arm around the girl's shoulders.

'You've never seen a pony up close before, have you, Emmy?'

She shook her head. 'But I want to. I've been thinking about it ever since you said we were coming here again.' She turned to Sophie, looking up at her, a serious look in her green eyes. 'Will we be able to ride them? I've ridden a donkey before, but I've never had a ride on a pony.'

'I think so,' Sophie said, 'as long as we keep to the main courtyard area. At least it's well lit, with all the security lighting. Let's see how you get on with them. They're used to children, because the children come from the village to ride them from time to time. They get very excited when that happens.'

'Who gets excited?' Lucas asked. 'The children?'

'Well, yes,' Sophie said with a smile, 'but actually I meant the ponies. They look forward to visitors. Just watch, and you'll see them come trotting up from the far end of the paddock.' She glanced at Emily. 'See, over there? They're coming to the fence to find out who's coming to see them.'

'I like the brown one,' William said, his eyes bright with excitement. 'He's the biggest and he has a big mane and a long tail. Can I ride him?'

'I should think so. I'll get a couple of riding

hats from the shed. You go over to the fence with Lucas while I sort out a couple of saddles and head collars.'

'Won't you need some help with those?' Lucas asked. 'I'm sure the children will be okay if I come and help you.'

'Just as long as they don't get too close to the ponies while we're not with them. Thanks, I could do with a hand. But tell William and Emily to keep their hands clear of the ponies until I have the chance to show them what to do.'

Lucas showed William and Emily how to stand back and simply look at the Shetlands while they waited for him and Sophie to bring the riding equipment. She glanced at them to make sure they were following instructions, and then led the way to the small shed by the stables. 'We keep everything in here,' she said, showing Lucas the way. Then she realised what she had said, and a sudden feeling of loss swamped her.

'You were thinking of your parents?' Lucas queried, a frown coming into his eyes.

'I… Yes… I keep forgetting,' she answered flatly. 'We worked as a team whenever we were together on the farm. It seems very bleak and strange without them. I'm finding it hard to get used to things the way they are now.'

He laid an arm around her. 'You're doing very well, though, holding things together, from what I can see.' He gazed around. 'This is a huge place. It's a lot for you to handle.'

'I suppose it is, but my parents loved it here, and I feel I owe it to them to keep it going.' She gave a rueful smile. 'Besides, the house sort of tugs at me. It's special, somehow…full of history, and every room holds memories of family life for me. I have to make it all work out.'

'Wouldn't Nathan have helped you with that?' Lucas's expression was sombre. 'From what you said, he seemed to be comfortable with the house and the farm.'

'Yes, he was, but, as I said, his plans were way out of line with what I had in mind. I think he wanted to change the whole nature of the place. It would have become a stud farm in the main, and a good part of the house would have been taken over as a veterinary practice—that's not what I had in mind at all. I prefer to keep it much the way it is now, as a family home. My parents worked for years to make it this way, and I grew up with it like this. I've been happy here.'

'But if you loved him, wouldn't you have gone along with what Nathan wanted?' He was watching her carefully, intent on her answer, and she wondered if he was trying to decide if she was in some way fickle.

Her gaze met his. 'If he loved me, wouldn't he have understood what was important to me?' She gave a helpless shrug. 'We could have worked together to build the veterinary practice if that was his ambition, but he didn't include me in his plans. He'd worked everything out to suit himself. It didn't occur to him that I might have other ideas, and when he did finally listen to me, he was a bit dismissive.' She frowned. 'I was living in the past, he said. It was time for change, time to move on, and I'm not ready for that.'

'I'm sorry.'

'Don't be.' After that, her illness had intervened, and Nathan's reaction had shown her that she should be forever wary about getting involved with any man. Her symptoms had shown no signs of going away, and she was beginning to believe that maybe it was something she was always going to be cursed with. What did that bode for future relationships?

It was best to steer clear, she decided. She could concentrate on her career, and put all her energies into that instead.

Keen to change the subject, she lifted down a saddle and handed it to him, along with a head collar. 'We'll put that one on Honeysuckle, and this one…' she hauled down another '…is for Daisy.'

He sent her an amused look. 'Honeysuckle?' he repeated.

'He's the chestnut with the honey-coloured mane and tail, and Daisy's brown with a silver mane and tail. They're both around five years old, and they're both very sweet natured.'

'I'm sure they are. They certainly look placid enough.'

They walked towards the fence, where they could see the children giggling and apparently talking to the ponies.

'He keeps putting his head through the fence

and nuzzling me,' William said, his voice filled with laughter.

'And this one tried to sniff me,' Emily put in. They both started to giggle all over again.

'That's because they know you have something in your pockets,' Sophie said, smiling. 'Perhaps we should give them each a carrot now. See how I do it, and then you can try.'

It was some time later, after riding the ponies a few times around the courtyard with Sophie and Lucas holding the lead reins, that the children were finally ready to get down, pat their new friends and say goodbye to them.

'Thank you for letting me ride you,' Emily said softly, leaning her head against Daisy. She cuddled her, and the pony made a soft whinnying sound.

'They like you,' Sophie said, looking at William and Emily. 'Perhaps you'll come back and see them again some time?'

'Yes, please. Can we?' William looked at Lucas, and he nodded.

'I think so. You've been really sensible and patient with them today. I think you've made two new friends.'

Sophie glanced at him as she stabled the ponies. 'You like being with the children, don't you? I know you felt a bit unsure of yourself about keeping them occupied, but you're really very good with them. I don't think you need have any worries on that score.'

His mouth curved. 'Well, I'm glad you think so.'

'I do.' She studied him thoughtfully. 'Have you ever thought about having a family of your own someday?'

He reflected on that for a moment or two and then shook his head. 'I never really gave it much thought. Up to now, I've enjoyed my freedom too much to think of settling down…and, to be honest, I think I probably prefer to leave the child-raising to my sister. She's very good at it.'

Sophie's expression was rueful. Perhaps she might have guessed his answer would be something along those lines. He certainly seemed at ease with all the attention he received from his female colleagues at work, and why would he want to give that up?

His gaze shifted, drifting over her. 'What about you? From what I've seen, you have a wonderful way with children—it's one of your most endearing qualities. I'm sure you'd be a natural as a mother.'

Sophie felt something clutch at her heart, and an instant feeling of tension gripped her. She longed to have children someday, but how could it happen if she could never manage to sustain a relationship? She only had to recall how disastrously things had turned out with Nathan to remind her of that.

'I don't know. I'm not sure that it will ever happen for me…but I love being with children, and perhaps I can get something of what I need through working with them. I feel more fulfilled when I'm on the children's ward. I just think that when you look at things through children's eyes, it opens up a whole new world, full of exciting possibilities.'

'I'm sure you're right.' He helped her as she finished putting away the saddles, and then she locked up and together they walked back to the house.

They went into the cosy farmhouse kitchen, where Sophie made milky drinks for the children and put on a pot of coffee for her and Lucas. 'When will Tom be back, do you know?' she asked him as she put out biscuits on a plate and pushed them across the table to William and Emily.

'Some time this evening. I'll take the children over to my parents' house in a while, and he'll collect them from there.'

Sophie glanced at William and Emily. 'If you've finished your drinks, would you like to spend some time in the playroom?' she asked. 'There are some toys in the big chest in there that you might not have seen.'

'Yes, please.' William was all for it, and Emily nodded, her eyes shining.

'Okay, I'll—'

She broke off as the phone rang, and Lucas said helpfully, 'I'll take them through to the playroom if you want to take your phone call.'

'Thanks.' She picked up the receiver and watched them go.

'Hello, Dr Mason,' she said a moment later. 'Is everything all right? I've not missed an appointment with you, have I?'

'No, my dear, nothing like that. I wanted to talk to you about your blood-test results.'

'Oh, yes. I was going to ring up and ask if you had them back from the lab. What is it? Have you managed to find out what's wrong with me?'

'Not exactly.' Dr Mason hesitated momentarily. He was in his late fifties, a kind man, who always had his patients' welfare at heart. He was a dedicated GP, and Sophie had always had the utmost respect for him. 'But it may be that your body's not utilising iron properly. Instead the iron stores could be building up in your tissues and causing problems, such as the tiredness and the joint pains you've been experiencing.'

Sophie frowned. 'But how could that be?'

'That's what we have to find out. At the moment, the blood tests are showing that something is not right.'

'So what needs to be done? Why is this happening?'

'We don't know yet. I think perhaps it would be best if I refer you to a specialist. I'm thinking you might have a condition called haemochromatosis, which basically means an overload of iron.' He paused. 'Did your parents suffer from the condition, do you know?'

Sophie was still struggling to take in the diagnosis. She was conscious of Lucas coming back into the room, but he remained silent while she was taking her phone call, going over to the worktop and retrieving his coffee.

'No,' she answered slowly. She felt for a chair and sat down, her legs feeling weak and strange all of a sudden. 'I don't believe so. My parents were extremely healthy. In fact, I hardly ever knew them to be ill.'

'Hmm.' Dr Mason was obviously thinking things over. 'That's interesting, because haemochromatosis is mainly an inherited disease. People who suffer from it where it isn't inherited are usually those who have been receiving long-term blood transfusions for other types of illness.' He appeared to shake off his thoughtful mood. 'Anyway, at the moment we don't know anything for sure and this is all supposition. We need to check things out, so if you would make an appointment with the practice nurse, she'll do what's necessary, and I'll get in touch with a specialist. That way we'll find out exactly what we're dealing with.'

'All right. I'll do that. I'll make an appointment for sometime this week. Thank you, Dr Mason. I appreciate you taking the time to call me.'

'You're welcome, Sophie. Don't worry, we'll get this sorted out.'

'Yes. Thank you. Goodbye.' She replaced the receiver on its cradle and stared into space for a moment or two.

'Was that bad news?' Lucas asked, pulling out a chair and coming to sit beside her.

'Um...no, it was nothing.' She was still trying to take it all in. How could she possibly have inherited a disease from her parents? Surely there must be some mistake?

'It didn't sound like nothing.' Lucas handed her a mug of coffee. 'Drink up, it will make you feel better.'

'I'm fine,' she said. 'There's nothing wrong with me.'

He reached out and laid his palm gently over her hand. 'Why don't you tell me what it's all about, Sophie?' he murmured. 'I know something's wrong. I can see it in your face. And you're deathly pale all of a sudden, as though you've had some kind of shock. Talk to me. Perhaps I can help.'

She shook her head. 'I don't need any help. I told you. I'm fine.'

He was watching her closely, and clearly he was puzzled by her refusal to open up to him, but she couldn't bring herself to confide in him. He'd helped her enough already, and if she carried on this way he would soon begin to think she was weak.

No, she would keep her troubles to herself. It was important that she stay independent, and she simply couldn't share her problems any more, even with someone as charismatic as Lucas.

CHAPTER FIVE

THE first flurries of snow fell over the Cotswold Hills as November advanced towards December. Sophie hurried into work and shook the damp droplets from her coat before hanging it up to dry in the changing room just off the children's ward.

'At this rate, we'll be looking forward to a white Christmas,' Hannah remarked, putting her own coat on the rail and walking with Sophie to the nurses' station.

'Heavens,' Sophie retorted with a laugh, 'I don't have time for Christmas. I've way too much to do. Do you think we could cancel it, just for this year?'

'Not on your life.' Hannah grinned. 'I love Christmas. I can't wait for it to come.' She looked Sophie over. 'I'll go and make a pot of coffee—that might help to cheer you up.'

'Yes, that should do the trick.' Sophie checked

through the pile of lab results in the wire tray, and then moved on to scan the patients' charts. She rubbed at her knuckles to ease the ache that had started up there, and then she frowned. It was the cold that was causing the pain in her hands, wasn't it? That had to be the answer. That would account for the nasty twinges she was getting in the rest of her joints, too. It was possible Dr Mason had been mistaken about her diagnosis, wasn't it? The results of the latest batch of tests hadn't come back from the lab yet.

Hannah handed her a mug of coffee, and she wrapped her hands around it, enjoying the warmth that permeated into her fingers. 'I'd better make a start on my rounds as soon as I've finished this,' she said. 'I see we had a couple of new admissions overnight, so I'll start with them. And young Marcus should be going home today. His condition's stable for the moment, so Mr Burnley said it would be okay to discharge him. He'll come back in for his operation some time next month.'

'Okay. I'll make the arrangements.'

From then on, the day progressed well enough,

but just as it was getting close to lunchtime, Sophie's pager bleeped and she hurried down to A and E.

'You have a patient for me?' she said, as soon as she came across Lucas in one of the side rooms.

'Yes...this five-year-old boy suddenly collapsed. I want to bring Debbie in on this one, but I hoped you would take a look at him before I call in a specialist. The child was brought here by ambulance a short time ago.'

His gaze travelled over her, but his expression was oddly remote, somehow withdrawn. His manner towards her had changed in a subtle fashion over these last few weeks, as though she had let him down in some way. She guessed he was disappointed in her. She knew he wanted her to confide in him, to trust him, but she hadn't been able to bring herself to do that, and now he was guarded in his dealings with her.

She missed the friendly banter that they had shared, and she knew the remedy lay in her own hands, but her life was in a state of flux at the moment, it was confusing, and she didn't want to add to the mistakes she had already made. How could she put her faith in anyone? Things had gone badly wrong with Nathan and then she'd had to face up to the biggest upset of all—the loss of her parents. She felt as though she had been deserted, as though she had cast out to sea and now she was being tossed about on a bleak ocean.

'His blood pressure's high,' Lucas went on. 'I believe it's due to intracranial pressure, but we need to find a cause.'

'Of course.' Sophie looked at the dark-haired child lying on the bed. His face was puffy, showing signs of oedema. He looked very ill. 'Have you done all the usual tests?'

He nodded. 'I've ordered blood tests, as well as a urinalysis for blood and protein, and I'm checking for plasma leaks of creatinine and urea. His urine dipstick test showed the presence of protein and microscopic amounts of blood.'

Sophie sucked in her breath. 'Poor little lad. It looks as though there's something going on with his kidneys.'

'Yes, that was my conclusion, too. His mother said he had a really bad sore throat prior to this.'

'It's beginning to sound as though we could be dealing with a streptococcal infection.' She briefly scanned the boy's chart. 'I suggest we treat the oedema with diuretics and keep a close eye on his potassium levels. And of course we need to manage his blood pressure very carefully.'

Lucas inclined his head briefly. 'We certainly need to bring the inflammation levels down as quickly as possible. I'm cautious about giving corticosteroids at this stage, because it's not likely they'll be effective. At any rate, we need a nephrologist's opinion, and in the meantime I'll prescribe penicillin as a precaution to eradicate any strep infection.'

'Yes, we should get somebody down here right away…and make arrangements to transfer him to the paediatric intensive care unit.' She looked at the child again. How could any mother bear to see her child suffering this way? And yet, for all the heartache she saw in her job as a paediatrician, there were moments of pure joy, elation, and it only strengthened the feeling that one day she would love to have children of her own. Would there ever be a time when the farmhouse would be filled with youngsters?

Her glance wandered, drifting to Lucas, strong, capable, kind and caring, everything you could want in a man. Would it be so much of a risk if she were to relax, just a little, and take comfort in his arms?

She batted the thought away almost as soon as it had come. It wouldn't do to think that way. Why would he want her—or, rather, why would he stay with her, when she was constantly tired and aching and in need of help and support? And, anyway, hadn't he implied that he was a confirmed bachelor?

'It's so sad to see children like this, isn't it?' she said. 'It's bad enough at any time, but when they're totally helpless it's really worrying, and we have our work cut out to try and discover what's brought it all on from any number of possibilities.'

'But you're very good at what you do, Sophie.' His gaze meshed with hers. 'I know if that were my child lying there, I'd trust you implicitly to do the right thing.'

She gave a rueful smile. 'That works both ways.' She hesitated momentarily, then added, 'I thought you were very good with William and Emily, by the way. You seem to be getting the hang of things, dealing with children.'

Lucas smiled as he wrote up the boy's medication on his chart and handed it to the nurse in attendance. 'We'll do fifteen minute observations, please,' he told her.

The nurse nodded agreement, and moved away to set up the medication.

Lucas turned back to Sophie. 'I've been getting quite a lot of practice lately with William and Emily. Ella's back home now, but she has to rest a lot, and I've been lending a hand whenever I can. I'm finding I quite enjoy it. They're a lively pair, and they keep me on my toes.' He checked the boy's blood pressure once more. 'In fact, I'm taking them into town later on today.' He looked at her cautiously, as though an idea was occurring to him. 'They want to find a present for their mother—it's her birthday next week—and Tom isn't able to go with them. He's been having a particularly difficult time at work lately.'

'It's lucky he's able to call on you, then.'

He nodded. 'I suppose so—though I'm not so sure I know how to advise the children on what to pick out for Ella.' His glance flickered over her. 'I don't suppose you'd care for a shopping trip this afternoon, would you? You have a half-day today, don't you? If I remember correctly, we're both booked in for a meeting that has been cancelled at the last minute, so as far as I can see we're both footloose and fancy-free.' His expression was hopeful, expectant.

Her heart gave a tiny, unexpected leap at the invitation. Clearly, he still wanted to spend time with her. 'Yes, that's right,' she said with a smile. It wasn't a date, but all the same her spirits lifted at the prospect of spending time with him. 'I think I could manage that and, anyway, I'd like to see William and Emily again.'

The door opened just then, and Debbie came to join them by the bedside. She nodded towards Sophie and then turned to Lucas. 'How is the boy doing?' she asked.

'Not so well,' he answered, his expression becoming sombre. 'Perhaps this is one case you should follow up for your exam studies. He'll be going over to Intensive Care later on—maybe you should go with him, and see him settled in.'

'I will.' Debbie smiled, and then reached in her pocket and handed Lucas a mobile phone. 'You left this at my place last night. I thought you might be needing it.'

Lucas peered at the phone. 'Good grief. I've been searching everywhere for that. Thanks, Debbie.'

'You're welcome.' She started to walk away towards the door. 'I have to get back to my trauma patient. Let me know when Jason is ready to go over to ICU.'

'I will.'

Sophie felt as though a tight band had clamped itself around her chest. He had been with Debbie last night? At her house? What was she to make of that?

It just went to show that her instincts had been right all along. Lucas had other interests, and she'd done the right thing, holding back from him. Yet now she'd messed it up by agreeing to go on a shopping trip with him. There was a hollow feeling in her stomach.

She frowned. No matter, there was nothing too intense about going into town with him. She had read too much into his invitation. She would simply be helping him out, and she would do her best to keep things on a light, friendly footing. She had meant it when she'd said she would like to see the children again. She'd go with him for their sakes.

'So,' Lucas said, turning to Sophie, 'shall I pick you up at the farmhouse at around one o'clock this afternoon?'

'That sounds fine to me,' she told him.

Still reeling from a feeling of shock, she went back to the children's ward a few minutes later, and helped to see Marcus off with his parents.

The little boy was sitting in his pushchair, and after a prompt from his mother he said, 'Thank you for looking after me.' He gave her an endearing smile. 'And thank you for helping me with my jigsaws. I liked them, 'specially the ones with the puppies and the kittens.'

'They were my favourites, too.' Sophie gave

him a hug, and saw him on his way. She would miss him, and she would worry about him, too. He was a brave little boy. The narrowing of his aorta was placing a great strain on his heart, leading to poor circulation, shortness of breath and chest pain, and a lot was riding on this operation that Mr Burnley was going to perform. It was an operation that could change the boy's life for ever.

She went home after her shift ended at lunchtime, and changed into jeans and a stretchy cotton top. Once Lucas arrived, she would add a sweater and jacket, and then she would be prepared for the cold weather outside. The ground was still frosty underfoot, so she put on black leather boots to complete the ensemble.

She made a swift circuit of the animal enclosures, making sure they were all safe and secure. 'Behave yourself while I'm out,' she told George the goat in a stern voice. 'And don't go chewing what's left of my Michaelmas daisies.' She patted Jessie on the flank and looked at her doubtfully. 'I'm going to have to do something about your diet,' she said. 'You're getting way too fat.' She certainly wasn't as active as George, and didn't seem to burn off the energy.

She finished tending to the animals just as the phone began to ring. She frowned. Was Lucas ringing to cancel? Despite her misgivings about the trip, she felt a sudden tide of disappointment wash through her. It didn't matter that he was seeing Debbie. She wanted to spend time with him, and she couldn't explain her reasoning, either to him or to herself.

'Hello, Sophie.' Dr Mason's warm, reassuring tones reached her from the other end of the line. 'I'm ringing to update you on what's happening, as I promised.'

'Oh, of course. I was thinking about that this morning. Thanks for getting back to me.'

'You're welcome. I've been talking to the haematologist,' he added, 'and he thinks it would be a good idea for you to make an appointment to have an ultrasound scan of your liver.'

Sophie reached for a chair and sat down. Instinctively she knew she needed to steel herself for this. 'You think I have something wrong with my liver?'

'Not necessarily, but if you do have haemochromatosis—an overload of iron—it could be that your liver may be involved in the process. We're just trying to eliminate possibilities at the moment.'

She felt dizzy all at once, and laid a hand on the table to steady herself. Dr Mason must have noted her silence, because he asked, 'Are you all right, Sophie?'

'Yes, I'm fine. Go on, please. Perhaps you could explain things to me a little more.' She'd been looking it up, of course, anxious to find information about the disease ever since he had first mentioned the possibility of it to her. Even so, she wanted to hear what he had to say.

'I will.' He was quiet for a moment. 'You're a doctor, so I expect you want more than just a simple explanation…would I be right in thinking that?'

'Yes…please. I want to know what I might be dealing with.'

'Well, and do bear in mind that nothing is certain as yet. As you probably know, when you absorb too much iron, it begins to be deposited in various parts of the body…the liver, the pancreas, joints, bone marrow, heart and even the endocrine glands. This can cause damage and lead to various conditions like cirrhosis of the liver or diabetes, arthritis and heart conditions.' He paused for a second or two. 'I know you've been suffering from pains in your joints and extreme tiredness, and even some abnormal heart rhythms from time to time, so it's probably safe to say that if you do have the disease, it will have been building up there from childhood.'

Sophie struggled to find her voice. 'Is there a cure? From what I've read about it, treatment involves taking blood—is there any other alternative?'

'Not really. There are tablets that will remove iron from the body, but they can be toxic and they tend not to be used much, except in certain circumstances. The usual course of action is for you to give blood every week for about a year until the condition settles. Taking just a pint of blood will cause iron to be released from the tissues where it was stored. After that the treatments can be done two or three times a year.'

Her tone was flat. 'So what does this mean for me?'

'At the moment, nothing, unfortunately. We have to wait for test results to come in. I can't start you on a treatment until we have a definitive answer.'

'I see.' Her mind was spinning as she tried to take the news on board. 'Thank you. Thank you for letting me know.' Her voice was faint. She was feeling slightly sick with shock to have learned that she had gone from being a fairly healthy individual to someone who might have a disease that was going to involve long-term interventions.

'I know this has been difficult for you to take in,' Dr Mason said. His voice was kind and sympathetic, and Sophie knew that he was sincere. 'Of course, in the meantime, there are things you can do to reduce the amount of iron you take in, through diet, for instance. Less red meat, no spinach, generally avoid foods containing iron wherever possible, and steer clear of vitamin C, because that helps with the absorption of iron in your body.'

'I'll remember that,' Sophie murmured. 'I'll try to work out a plan of what I should eat or not eat.'

'We'll get you some help with that. The important thing is that you shouldn't worry about any of this,' Dr Mason said. 'If we're right about the diagnosis, we can't cure you, but we can treat the disease, and before too long you should start to feel much better.'

'I understand. Thank you.'

She cut the call a minute or so later, and sat for some time trying to come to terms with what the doctor had told her. It was an alien situation she found herself in, and she wasn't sure what to make of it right now.

She didn't have long to dwell on things, though, because the doorbell rang a short time later, and from the animated sound of children's voices, she realised that Lucas had arrived with his niece and nephew.

He looked at her oddly as she greeted him and showed the way towards the kitchen. 'What's up, Sophie?' he asked, and she winced inwardly at his unerring perception. 'Have you changed your mind about going into town with us?'

'No, not at all,' she answered. 'I have a few things on my mind, that's all, but it's nothing for you to worry about.'

To distract him she put on a cheerful face and bent down to adddress the children. 'You can go and say hello to Honeysuckle and Daisy, if you like,' she told them. 'I'll cut a couple of apples into halves, if you want to give them a treat.'

'Woo-hoo!' William exclaimed a moment later, accepting the apple and running out to the paddock, leaving his sister to follow eagerly in his wake.

'Have you thought some more about what you want to buy for Ella?' she asked Lucas as she went to retrieve her sweater from the back of a chair in the kitchen.

'I thought I might get her a necklace and earring set that she's been hankering after. She's been complaining of looking like a blimp, with her baby bump and the increase in her weight, and no matter how much we try to convince her that she looks great, she's convinced herself otherwise and she's thoroughly out of sorts. I guess a bit of luxury might make her feel much more feminine.' He smiled. 'As to what the children might get for her, I haven't a clue. William's talking about bath oils and soaps, but Emily's not sure.'

Sophie lifted her sweater from the chair and paused to ease her aching shoulders, moving them slowly in a circular motion to ease the stiff muscles. Lucas's gaze narrowed on her.

'You're still very pale,' he said, 'and it looks as though your aches and pains are still there. Hasn't the doctor come up with a treatment plan yet? I know you've been to see him.'

She pulled a face. Her illness wasn't something she wanted to share with the world, but Lucas had always been thoughtful and caring, and she was beginning to realise that he wouldn't rest until he had found out what was going on.

'It's taking a while for my GP to find out what's wrong with me,' she said with a sigh, 'because it isn't straightforward. There are a number of illnesses that can cause joint pain. But he phoned me, just a few minutes ago, to say that he and the specialist want to do more tests. It could be that I've been storing iron in my tissues for several years, and that's what's causing the trouble. The only treatment is to give blood on a regular basis.'

Lucas frowned. 'That sounds like a pretty drastic solution.' He studied her features, and she guessed he was seeing the lines of strain in her face and the shadows of weariness that showed beneath her eyes. 'It must have come as a huge shock to you—it's not the kind of diagnosis you hear every day, is it? Or one that you would ever want to hear?'

She shook her head, and the silky, golden tendrils of her hair drifted momentarily and then settled on her shoulders. 'No, but, then, we don't know yet if that *is* the problem.' She pulled in a deep breath and straightened up. 'Do you mind if we don't talk about it? I need time to think things through, and I'm just not ready to go into it at the moment.' She frowned, a sudden thought occurring to her. 'And please don't talk to anyone at work about this. I don't want people thinking I'm not up to my job. That's not true at all. I can do my work perfectly well. I can handle things.'

Lucas nodded, but she saw him glance around the farmhouse kitchen and look through the window to the paddock beyond and to the meadows, and the rows of polythene tunnels, all with plants that needed tending. She knew what he was thinking. How on earth could she carry on when there was so much to be done?

'I do have help around the place,' she said. 'There's a farm manager who sees to all the planting and the gathering in of the crops. I collected some of the fruit this season because he had to take time off for a domestic emergency and there was a problem with his stand-in. And this last couple of weeks I've managed to find a couple of teenagers who will come in every day to help with the animals. So, with any luck, things should start to ease up for me.'

'That's something, at least.' He came to stand beside her, and laid his hands lightly on her shoulders, caressing her gently as though he would take the pain from her and absorb it into himself. 'I worry about you,' he said. 'I wish you would let me help you. If there is anything I can do, anything at all, you only have to ask.'

'You're very good to me,' she said softly. 'It isn't that I don't appreciate the offer. It's just that I'm not used to relying on people. Even with my parents around, I nearly always tried to sort things out for myself, because I knew they were busy. I know they would have done anything for me, but I didn't want to burden them. And…' she hesitated '…it bothers me, having to ask for help. The one time I turned to Nathan for help and advice and sympathy, I found that he wasn't there for me at all…not in the way that I needed him.'

She looked into Lucas's eyes. 'So…I think what I'm trying to say—and perhaps I'm not making a very good job of it—is that it's really hard for me to open up and let people in. I feel as though I've been knocked to the ground, first with what happened to my parents and then with Nathan. I'm trying to get back on my feet, but it's taking some time.'

'It doesn't help that you're ill,' Lucas said. 'How can you hope to feel on top of the world when you're sick? I wish there was something I could do to take the burden away from you.' He drew her close to him, running his hand along her spine, making her feel cherished, wanted. Unexpectedly, the gesture brought tears to her eyes. They were tears of frustration, perhaps, of longing and an unspoken need that could not be satisfied.

The kitchen door burst open and the children tumbled into the room. Lucas and Sophie broke apart, and Lucas said in a determinedly cheerful voice, 'Perhaps a little retail therapy is in order. Maybe it's time we hit the town.'

Sophie nodded, pulling herself together and shepherding the children towards the door and Lucas's car.

They set off for the town centre, some five or six miles away, and when they finally arrived and parked up Sophie was startled to see that the window displays were already showing Christmas themes, with lots of red and gold and shot through with glitter and sparkle. 'I expect they'll be switching on the Christmas lights before too long,' she said.

In the main shopping centre, the seasonal theme was already in full swing. An inviting

Santa's grotto had been prepared, amidst a beautiful winter wonderland scene. There was a log cabin covered in thick, white, artificial snow and surrounded by fir trees glistening with sparkling frost, ready for the children to go and visit the magical figure. Inside the grotto, Sophie could see a warm red glow, and festive sacks brimming full of toys that Santa would give to the youngsters who came and sat on his knee and confided their secret wishes. Outside, his reindeer waited patiently, guarding the sleigh that was loaded with brightly coloured packages of all shapes and sizes.

'Look,' William said in an awed voice, 'I can see Santa's helpers.' Eyes shining, he was gazing at an animated display, a moving tableau of pixies and elves, busy making toy trains, dolls, musical boxes and all manner of delightful playthings.

Emily tugged at Lucas's hand. 'Can we go and see them?' she asked in a small voice.

'Of course you can.' He smiled down at her and urged her forward, but she wouldn't let go of his hand.

'I want you to come with me,' she said, drawing

him along with her. She was obviously overcome with wonder at the sight, but she was too afraid to venture any closer without him.

William had no such qualms. He walked forward and started to tell the elves all about his Christmas wish list. 'Do you think you could make me a big, big truck?' he said. 'A red one…I like red. And a castle, so that I can play with my toy soldiers and they can stand at the windows and shoot the enemy.' He didn't seem to mind that the elves didn't answer him. It was enough for him that the whole atmosphere was filled with enchantment.

Emily gazed around her, taking it all in. 'They have to work ever so hard,' she said. 'They have to make all the toys in all the world for all the children.'

'They do,' Lucas agreed. 'Santa needs them, if he's to fill his sleigh with toys.'

They stayed at the grotto for quite a while, and William and Emily in turn went to see Santa and receive a gift.

'What did you get?' Sophie asked William.

'It's a red racing car,' he said. 'Brmm, brmm.'

The car made wide circles in the air as he pretended to run it along an imaginary racetrack.

Emily carefully opened her package. 'It's a speckledy hen,' she said, showing it to Sophie, her eyes widening.

'Oh, my,' Sophie said, smiling. 'I remember having one of those when I was little. You press it down on a tabletop, or the floor, and it lays an egg.'

Emily tried it out on a nearby shelf, exclaiming gleefully when the russet-coloured hen produced an egg. 'Is it a real chocolate one?' she asked. 'Is it all right to eat it?'

Lucas nodded. 'It looks as though you have quite a few in that little bag. Perhaps you could let your brother have a taste?'

Emily obliged readily enough, and Sophie warned her gently, 'Perhaps you'd better save one or two so that your hen can go on laying them.'

'I will.'

Lucas laid a hand lightly on Sophie's waist as they left the grotto and prepared to wander around the shops. He looked at her with affection, and there was an easy familiarity between them, a comfortable feeling of togetherness. She liked the warmth of his fingers gliding down to rest on the curve of her hip. It was a gesture that came naturally to him. His was a hands-on, tactile personality and he probably hadn't given it a second thought.

It didn't take long for William to choose his mother's present. Soaps and bath oils were abandoned in favour of a pretty, mirrored jewellery box with a delicate, enamelled flower design painted on the front. Emily took her time. She wanted to get it right, and Lucas was very patient with her, helping her to choose by offering suggestions here and there.

She listened carefully and then pushed them all to one side. 'I want to get her a photo frame,' she said. 'One that's got lots of spaces for different pictures. She said she wanted one. She said she wants to put the whole family into the one photo frame so we need five spaces altogether—that will leave one for when the baby's born.'

Sophie was thoughtful for a moment. 'I saw some pretty silver ones last time I came into town,' she said. 'Let's go and see if we can find them, and then you can choose.'

She hoped Emily would soon make up her mind. It felt as though it had been a long day, and she was beginning to flag a little. Lucas's arm tightened around her, supporting her, and she guessed he knew exactly how she was feeling.

'It shouldn't take too much longer,' he murmured, and then frowned. 'Perhaps I shouldn't have landed you with this. You should have been resting, but I didn't realise the illness was weighing you down so much. It's hard to get used to the idea that something really is wrong.'

'It isn't that bad,' she said in a quiet voice. 'It crept up on me gradually, and it took me a while to accept that I needed to get it sorted out. At least now I know a little bit about what I'm dealing with.'

He nodded and hugged her closer to him.

'I like that one,' Emily said at last, choosing a picture frame that had a decorative motif in one corner made up of small, faceted glass beads.

'It's beautiful. I'm sure she'll love it,' Sophie told her, glancing at Lucas.

'Definitely,' he agreed, smiling. 'We'll find some photos of you and William to put in it, if you like, to start off the display.'

Emily beamed her delight, and once the sales assistant had wrapped up her purchase and put it safely into her hands, they set off along the street once more.

'I think we should go and get a drink and something to eat at a café,' Lucas said, sending a swift glance over Sophie as he led the way towards a brightly lit coffee shop. 'It will give you the chance to rest a while,' he murmured. 'One way and another, it's been quite a day for you, hasn't it? You only heard from your GP just before we came out, and what he said must be playing on your mind. You've done well to put on such a brave front.'

He pushed open the door and they trooped inside. William chose a seat by the window and immediately sat down and began to run his car along the tabletop. Emily's hen started to deliver eggs at a regular rate.

Sophie sat down and reached for a menu. She might have known that Lucas would notice the determined effort she had been making. She nodded. 'I think it's all just beginning to catch up with me,' she said. 'And perhaps the thought of Christmas is something else I need to come to terms with. I've not been into town for a while, and seeing all the preparations has brought it home to me that it's not very far off.'

'Yes, I can see how it would give you a bit of a jolt. I suppose it's going to be very different for you this year.' He came and sat beside her.

The waitress walked over to the table and took their order—milkshakes and sticky buns for the children, coffee and toasted sandwiches for Lucas and Sophie.

'Have you made any arrangements yet?' Lucas asked. 'Will you be going away to spend time with friends this year?'

'I'm not sure. One of my friends has invited me to share Christmas with her and her family. I'm thinking it through, but I know she'll have a lot on her plate with the children and her husband's family coming to visit on the day.'

She reached for her coffee as the waitress placed it on the table. 'Christmas was always very special time for us at the farm,' she said, stirring sugar into the hot drink. 'We'd feed the animals early, and make sure they had special treats and warm bedding, and then we'd sit by the Christmas tree in the living room and try to guess what was in our parcels.' She smiled. 'It was funny, because my dad would always have slippers as one of his presents, come what may, because it was a kind of tradition. Last year, my mum bought him a pair with musical reindeer on the front, and all day long we'd hear choruses of "Rudolph, the Red-nosed Reindeer" coming from different parts of the house.'

Lucas chuckled. 'I've always loved that time of year,' he murmured. 'We don't do anything special, but the whole family gets together on Christmas Day. That's what makes it so great. We all start off by opening presents, and then we have dinner and talk or sit watching TV in the afternoon. We're usually too full up with roast turkey and Christmas pudding and wine to be able to do much more. Tom sometimes suggests a walk in the afternoon, and he and Ella might wander off for a while. William and Emily usually want to go on playing with their toys.'

'I suppose we were much the same,' Sophie said in a quiet voice. 'I can't imagine how it will be without them.'

He reached out and clasped her hand. 'That's why you need to be with friends,' he said. 'You could come over to my family, you know. I'd love to have you there. Ella wants to meet you, and you already get on very well with the children. My parents will be really pleased to see you. They'll welcome you like one of the family.'

Sophie felt a lump form in her throat. She wasn't sure what to say to him. Despite what he said, wasn't he simply being kind, wasn't he inviting her purely because he felt sorry for her? She didn't want that. She didn't want his pity or his sympathy, she wanted… What did she want from him…warm, deep, everlasting emotions? That wasn't going to happen, was it?

'Thank you. But I'll be all right, really.' Carefully she drew her hand away from his and made a pretence of being absorbed in her coffee.

He frowned, glancing at her briefly as though he was trying to fathom what she was thinking.

They finished their drinks and snacks, and then wandered around a few more shops before finally making their way back to the car. 'If you want to stop off at the farmhouse for a while,' she suggested to Lucas, 'the children could wrap their presents there. I keep a stock of wrapping paper in the study, and labels and tape that they can use. It will save them having to do it surreptitiously at their house.'

He gave her an affectionate squeeze as he helped her into the car. 'You think of everything,' he said, stooping to drop a kiss lightly on her mouth.

Sophie stared at him, her lips parting in startled reaction. She could feel that kiss tingling on her lips even as he moved away and carefully closed the passenger side door.

'You just kissed Sophie!' William said in a voice squeaky with scandalised surprise from the back seat, his eyes growing large. 'I saw you. I did.'

Emily giggled, clamping her hands over her mouth.

Sophie's cheeks grew hot. 'Now see what you've done,' she muttered, shooting a glance at Lucas as he slid into the driver's seat.

He chuckled, and cast an eye over the children. 'Well, she's an amazing person,' he said, as if that explained everything. 'See how she helped you to find just what you wanted for your mother? She's an angel.' He nodded towards the seat belts. 'Now, buckle up, everyone. It's time we were setting off.'

At the farmhouse, Sophie made sure that everyone warmed up by the fire in the living room, while she went into the study to search through the bureau for wrapping paper and tape. 'Perhaps you could flick the switch on the percolator in the kitchen,' she suggested, when Lucas would have followed her. 'The children should be safe enough in there on their own—there's a good, sturdy fireguard in place, and they seem preoccupied for the moment, playing with their new toys.'

'I'll do that.' He went off into the kitchen, leaving Sophie to rummage through the drawers.

The paper was always kept in the same place, in one of the large drawers at the bottom of the bureau, and so she found that easily enough. But then she discovered that the tape dispenser was empty, and she had to search for a new reel in the upper drawers, which contained most of the family papers.

They were all in a mess. She found the tape pushed in among various invoices, receipts and so on that had been stuffed higgledy-piggledy into the drawers, and sighed. She couldn't put off sorting through the paperwork for much longer. Her solicitor had been advising her that some documents needed her signature, and she really ought to see that everything was in order before too much longer.

'Here's the wrapping paper, some scissors and tape,' she told the children, going back into the living room. 'And there are a couple of pens and some labels for you. Do you think you'll be able to manage on your own for a little while, while I go and tidy up the mess I've made? If not, leave it until I can come and help you in a few minutes.'

They both nodded and seized on the coloured wrapping paper with enthusiasm. Sophie left them to it and went back to the bureau and started to tidy the papers into orderly piles.

'I took some mugs of hot chocolate into the living room for the children,' Lucas said, coming to join her a short time later. 'They seem to be managing quite well with the wrapping. Emily's taken over with writing the labels, and William is going to add his name and some kisses.'

She smiled up at him. 'That sounds about right,' she said.

He handed her a mug of coffee. 'It looks as though you have quite a bit of sorting out to do. Is there anything I can do to help?'

She shook her head. 'I don't think so. I didn't intend to tidy it up now, but I was sidetracked, looking for the tape. I'd forgotten how many of the family's household accounts were stored in here.'

Lucas was inspecting the bureau curiously. 'This is a fine piece of workmanship,' he said. 'I believe it's Edwardian. It's certainly beautifully crafted.'

She nodded. 'I've always liked it. I think it was handed down to my mother from her grandmother.'

'Did you ever find the secret drawer?' he asked, and she looked at him blankly.

'Secret drawer?' she echoed. She shook her head. 'I don't know what you mean.'

'There's often a secret drawer,' he murmured. 'May I?' He put out a hand to feel the indentations in the wood, beneath the second shelf.

She nodded. 'Go ahead. Be my guest.'

He pressed something, and a thin, small drawer shot out. He smiled his satisfaction. 'There you are,' he said with a smile. 'The not-so-secret drawer.'

Sophie stared at the rectangular box. 'There are some papers in there,' she said, a note of puzzlement in her voice. She drew the papers out and began to look at them, and after a moment or two, as she realised exactly what she was seeing, every bit of colour drained from her face.

'What is it?' Lucas asked. 'What have you found?'

'I… It's a certificate,' she said, her voice cracking with strain. 'And a couple of documents.' She didn't know what to do, or how to handle the information she read in those papers, and she handed them to him, unable to speak all at once, alarmed to realise that her hand was shaking violently.

Lucas studied the papers and then stared at her in consternation. He looked from her to the papers and back again. 'Sophie, I'm so sorry. I never would have dreamed— I'm so sorry.'

'I don't know what to make of it,' she said. 'Surely it can't be possible?' She swallowed hard against a sudden dryness in her throat. 'It's what I think it is, then?' She stared at him, her eyes wide and bewildered. Her head was beginning to throb and a pulse was hammering wildly in her throat. 'I hoped you would tell me that it isn't true.'

'I don't know what to say.' His voice was husky with emotion, and he wrapped his arms around her, comforting her as best he could. 'You've never seen those papers before?'

'No.' Her voice broke on a sob, and her eyes were suddenly awash with tears. 'I've never seen my birth certificate before. I never needed to. My mother dealt with anything that cropped up because I was busy and she wanted to help…at least, that's the reason she gave me.'

She tried to blink the tears away, but more came, and now they were flowing and she didn't know how to stop them from streaming down her face. 'If I'm not their daughter, then who am I?' she whispered.

'You *are* their daughter—it just means they adopted you, that's all. It's a shock, I know, but it doesn't mean it's a bad thing. It'll be all right, Sophie, believe me.' He stroked her hair, and a moment or two later his lips brushed her temples and she felt the warmth of that kiss shimmer through her whole body.

She wanted to believe him. She was glad that his arms were around her, keeping her safe. But none of this was going to turn out well, was it? She knew it through her grief and pain, and his deep felt concern couldn't do anything to take away the depth of her sorrow. Her whole life had been turned upside down.

CHAPTER SIX

'HOW are you, today, Jason?' Sophie glanced at the five-year-old. There was still some slight puffiness about his face, but in general he looked a whole lot better than he had done when she'd first seen him down in A and E some days ago. She checked his blood pressure and noted the reading down on his chart.

These last few days she had been trying to go on with her job at the hospital as though everything in her life was completely normal, as though everything she believed in hadn't been shaken to its foundations. Lucas had held her and comforted her, but even he hadn't been able to coax her out of her state of shock. She hadn't known what to do, or which way to turn.

At least the pace of life at the hospital meant that she had little time to dwell on her own problems.

Jason lifted his thin shoulders. 'I'm all right.'

He frowned and added in a disgruntled tone, 'But I don't like the food here. It's boring, and they don't let me have any salt with it.' His bottom lip jutted.

Sophie smiled. It was good to see that at least he cared about what he was eating. That hadn't been the case a while back when she'd gone to visit him in Intensive Care. Back then, he'd been too ill to pay any attention to what had been going on around him. The streptococcal infection had caused the glomeruli, the tiny blood vessels in his kidneys, to become inflamed, leaving his kidneys less able to do their job of filtering waste products. That had left his body in a toxic state.

'I'll ask the dietician to come and talk to you,' she said. 'She's the lady who knows all about food and what's good to eat. Perhaps she can help to find something that you'd like, something that's good for you at the same time.'

His brows lifted in surprise as he tried to take that in. 'Will you?' He looked pleased.

'Yes, I will. The thing is,' Sophie explained, 'we're trying to keep you off salt for a while, because it will make you poorly.'

'I've already been poorly.' Jason pulled a face and added, 'But now I want to go home. Can I go home soon?' His dark hair fell across his forehead in an unruly wave, and she had to resist the urge to gently push it back into place and soothe away his troubled frown.

'Of course you do.' The child had been very ill, but at least now they'd been able to transfer him from Intensive Care to the children's ward, much to his mother's delight. 'You're doing very well now, and I'm very pleased with you, but we just need to keep you in hospital for a little bit longer to make sure that everything is as it should be.' She was thoughtful for a moment or two. 'I'll ask Amy if she'll come along and find something to keep you amused—maybe a video game, or a puzzle, something that you can do in bed, because you really need to rest for a while and get your strength back.'

'Okay,' he said, brightening a little. 'I like Amy. She gave me a colouring book. I like colouring, but one of the cleaning ladies must have taken the book away, and I don't know where it is any more.'

'I'll see if I can find it for you,' Sophie said. 'Failing that, perhaps I could get you another one, would that do?'

He nodded eagerly. 'Yes, please.'

She left the bedside and went over to the nurses' station and rummaged around for a while in a cupboard below the counter.

'Have you lost something?' Lucas's deep voice sounded from above and she looked up to see him standing by the desk. For a moment, her heart skipped a beat. He was strong and well muscled, dressed immaculately in dark trousers and a crisp shirt finished off with a plain, stylish tie. He was impressively good looking, and in spite of herself her whole body went into meltdown.

Belatedly, she realised he was waiting for an answer. 'No,' she said, pulling herself together. 'I've found it. I've just the thing to set my patient back on the road to recovery.' Triumphantly, she produced a colouring book full of pictures of castles, wizards and fire-breathing dragons.

'Well, that'll certainly do the trick.' Lucas smiled briefly, and then his features settled into the guarded expression that she had come to know of late. He'd begun to tread lightly around her, this last week, and she guessed he was cautious about upsetting her in any way. 'Would it be okay if we talk for a while as soon as you've dispensed the medicine? I left it till nearly lunchtime before coming to find you, in the hope that you'd have some free time.'

She stood up, and nodded. 'Of course. You don't need to ask. I'm always glad to spend time with you.' Her mouth curved. 'I'll just give this to Jason,' she said.

Jason's worries evaporated as though the sun had come out when she handed him the book. 'Here are your pencils,' she said, lifting a box out of the bedside drawer. 'I'll come and have a look at you a little bit later and see how you're getting on.'

Jason nodded, but he was already turning the pages of the book to find a picture that he liked best of all.

'It sounds as though he's recovering nicely,' Lucas commented when she joined him once more by the desk. 'Is his blood pressure under control?'

'Yes. We should soon be able to take him off the drug and monitor him to see how well he does without it. He's still on the antibiotic, and we're concentrating on supportive treatment, watching his fluid intake, and so on. He's on a low-protein diet to decrease the kidneys' workload, and we're making sure he has complex carbohydrates to make up the calories.' Her mouth made a crooked shape. 'The trouble is, he doesn't care for brown pasta and brown rice, or fruit and vegetables, so we have bit of a problem there.'

He smiled. 'I can see that would be difficult.' He studied her features, his gaze lingering on the pale sweep of her cheekbones and the faint shadows beneath her eyes. 'How are things with you? I know you've been struggling to get over the shock of finding out you were adopted. It can't be easy for you…but you know I'm here for you, don't you, and that I'll help you through this in any way I can?'

'Yes, I know. It's really good of you. It means a lot to me, knowing that.'

He hadn't wanted to leave her that evening when she'd discovered her birth certificate in the drawer, but after a while, once she'd recovered after the initial trauma, she'd persuaded him that Ella would be worrying about the children if he didn't take them home. Even then, he had been ready to phone his sister and delay his return, but Sophie had refused to consider it.

Then, to add to her concerns, Nathan had turned up just as she had been seeing Lucas out. She hadn't had it in her to turn him away, and Lucas had clearly been disturbed about that.

Since then, Lucas had been a bit edgy about what was going on. Perhaps he remembered the first evening they'd met, when he'd rescued her—but now it must seem to him that his rescue had been in vain, because Nathan was eager to put things right between them and she appeared to be more confused than ever.

'Have you spoken to anyone about it?' Lucas asked, now, cutting into her thoughts.

She came back to the present with a start. 'About the adoption, you mean?'

He nodded.

'Yes, I had a brief conversation with the adoption agency.' She straightened her shoulders, bracing herself.

'What did they say? Were they willing to talk to you?' Lucas was tense all at once, his grey eyes smoky and troubled. 'I would have gone with you, if you had told me. I would have been there to give you some back-up, some support.' Perhaps he was put out because she'd not asked for his help.

'Yes, I guessed you would…' She smiled at him. 'But it was something I felt I needed to do alone.' She laid a hand lightly on his, and then withdrew it after a moment because that small, intimate gesture made her think about what might have been had she not been so wary about getting involved. Part of her longed to have him hold her once again, but another part sounded warning bells in her head.

There was too much going on in her life right now, and she was struggling to make sense of any of it. Lucas was an added complication. Her instincts were crying out to her to turn to him, but everything that had gone before told her to steer clear. There had been enough upset in her life. She couldn't take any more.

'Apparently I was adopted at around eighteen months old—the woman at the agency was surprised I hadn't been told.' She shook her head. 'I don't know why my parents couldn't have told me when I was young…wouldn't they have known how much of a shock this would be to me? Why on earth wouldn't they tell me?'

'Perhaps they thought you would reject them and go in search of your natural parents.'

'Well, it backfired on them because that's exactly how I feel right now…I want to know who I am. I'm hurt and upset, because they let me down by not being honest with me, and now there are so many questions in my mind that need answering. It's as though everything that went before was a lie. I still can't get my head around it.'

'It's bound to take time. You shouldn't judge them while your emotions are in upheaval. Give yourself a little longer to take it all in.'

She pressed her lips together briefly. 'I know what you're saying is sound sense, it's just that I feel so wound up about it. I should have suspected something when Dr Mason said my illness is an inherited one. Perhaps I didn't want to believe it. Now I'm full of questions about who my real parents are, and whether they are ill, too. It's all crowding in on me, and sometimes I feel as though my head's about to explode.'

'Perhaps you should be the one taking blood-pressure medication,' he said with a smile. 'You need to calm down a bit. You've enough on your plate without all this.'

'That's what Nathan said.' Her thoughts were far away for a moment or two, but she felt Lucas stiffen beside her, and realised that it had been a mistake to mention him.

'Are you and he seeing each other again?' He was tense, his whole body rigid, as though her answer really mattered to him.

'No…at least, not like we were before. I'm not sure what to do about the situation. He was ambitious and got a bit carried away before, and forgot that he needed to share things with me and try to understand my feelings, but now he seems to have come to his senses. He said he'd been foolish and thoughtless, and he wants to make amends.'

Lucas's jaw clamped. 'Haven't you been through enough already, with him? If you encourage him, you'll be back where you started.'

Her chin lifted. 'I'm not encouraging him. He has to come round to the farm every now and again—he's a vet. It's his job to see to the animals.'

'He can't be the only one at the veterinary practice. You could ask them to send someone else.'

'I don't see why I should have to do that.' She frowned. 'I'm not going to go around avoiding him. We're both sensible adults. I don't see any reason why we shouldn't try to get along amicably.'

Lucas sucked in air through his teeth, and it looked as though he was about to say something else when his pager started to bleep. He muttered an inaudible curse and checked the text message. 'I have to go,' he said, adding as a parting shot, 'You should take care you don't land yourself in even deeper waters. You've been down that road before and it led to chaos.'

'I can take care of myself,' she said.

'So you say.' Lucas strode away from her and she felt an instant stirring of regret in the pit of her stomach. Why was he so angry with her? She couldn't help the way she felt. Why should she change just because he expected it of her?

She was still in a quandary when she left work later that day. The situation with her parents, with Nathan, with Lucas was playing over and over again in her mind. She would have to find her natural parents. There would be no peace until she knew everything there was to know about them.

She woke up the following morning, a cold December day, and drew the bedroom curtains back to find that overnight a blanket of snow had covered the ground. It clung to the branches of the trees and lay on the rooftops, so that the outbuildings and meadows had a picture-postcard quality to them.

At least she didn't have to go to work in this. It was the weekend, and she had the day off, so for once there would be time to catch up on all her chores as well as tend to the animals. She did her rounds on the farm first, and spent the morning finishing off odd jobs.

Feeling restless, she put on boots and a coat and scarf and set off to walk along the country lane that led from the farmhouse to the village. Perhaps a brisk walk would help to clear her head. She was troubled about Lucas's reaction the previous day. Had she been too sharp with him? He was only trying to help, and he deserved better from her, surely? Then an errant thought struck her and she frowned. Why would he be so concerned about her seeing Nathan if he was involved with Debbie?

It hadn't been a one-off, him spending the evening with Debbie outside work. Debbie had told her how they'd had supper together just a couple of days ago. She had come over to the children's ward to see Jason, following up on his case for her studies, and that's when she had let it slip that she'd been seeing Lucas. Sophie tried not to let it bother her, but it niggled away in the background, upsetting her, and she didn't know what to make of her feelings. What else could she expect of Lucas, if she kept turning him away?

She trudged onwards through the snow. It was a long lane, and she was surrounded by fields and mature trees, all glorious in their stark winter guise. Coming to a rustic stile, she climbed up and sat for a moment on the fence, looking around. What was she doing, wearing herself out with the upkeep of a 17th-century house and all the farm land that went along with it? What had once been like an essential part of her was now false, and it seemed that all her life had been a sham.

She looked up as she heard someone approaching. 'I'm glad you stopped here,' Lucas said, rounding a bend in the lane and coming over to the stile. 'I called at the house, but a man walking his dog saw me and said you were headed this way.'

'Oh, you startled me.' Sophie's heart did a small flip in her chest. Her spirits lifted all at once, and she slid down from the fence and went to greet him. 'I wasn't sure whether or not you would be working today.'

He shook his head. 'I have the weekend off.' He gazed at her, taking in the pink of her cheeks, which were still flushed from her brisk walk. 'I wanted to see you. We didn't have time to finish our conversation yesterday, and it's been playing on my mind ever since. You've been out of sorts lately, and that's hardly surprising, given what's been going on. You must be going over everything in your mind, every conversation with your parents, every holiday together, every Christmas celebration.'

'Yes, that's true. I can't seem to stop myself from doing that.' She started to walk along the lane once more, and he fell into step beside her. 'I'm stunned by what happened,' she said. 'There's no other word for it. If I hadn't found that certificate in the drawer, I might have gone on in ignorance for years to come.' She pulled a face. 'Sometimes I wish it could have been that way, but there's no going back now.'

Lucas frowned. 'I feel that I'm to blame for that. If I hadn't found the hidden drawer—if I hadn't pointed it out to you—you'd still be blissful in your ignorance.'

She shook her head. 'I dare say I would have found out, sooner or later. Anyway, what's done is done. At least it's concentrated my mind. I realise now that I don't have any interest in keeping things going, back at the house. I might as well sell up and move on. I'll miss the animals, of course, but I'm sure I'll be able to find good homes for all of them.'

He gave her an incredulous stare. 'I can't believe I'm hearing you say that. How can you even think it? The farm has been your home all your life. How can you just turn your back on it? You love the place.'

'I don't feel right there any more. Everything that's gone before has been based on a lie. Why am I wasting my energy, struggling to keep it going, when it's not my true heritage?' She gave a heavy sigh. 'I'm thinking I'll go and see an estate agent some time next week and put it on the market.'

'You're not serious?' He looked shocked. 'You can't mean to throw it all away?'

'It's how I feel. It's what I think I should do. I don't belong here any more.' She suddenly shivered. 'I think I should turn back now. It's colder than I thought out here.'

'Here, let me warm you.' He wrapped his arms around her and began to chafe her back and sides with his hands until the heat began to tingle through her veins. It wasn't just his actions that made the blood start to race through her body, though, it was the fact that she was so close to him. That her soft curves were crushed against his strong, muscular frame, and every part of her started to pulse with an unaccountable longing. She realised that she wanted him to go on holding her. She wanted to preserve this moment for all time.

'Is that better?' he asked softly, and there was a faint roughness about his voice.

'Yes,' she said. 'Much better.' She looked up at him, and a silent moment of awareness passed between them. The air crackled with tension, and then she was conscious of his head lowering, coming closer and closer. His gaze locked with hers, his eyes smoky, turbulent, filled with promise.

She tilted her head a little, her lips parting in breathless expectation, waiting for that kiss. And when it came, it was everything she could ever have dreamed of. His mouth claimed hers, lightly pressuring her, tasting her, turning her lips to flame and taking everything she had to offer.

It was a wonderful, exhilarating sensation and she revelled in that delicious coming together. He coaxed a response from her and she gave it willingly, losing all reason, all sense of time and place. His kiss tantalised and excited her and she wanted it to go on and on. For once, she felt safe and secure, as though she was home at last.

'I've wanted to do this for so long,' he whispered. 'I can't be with you without wanting to take you into my arms. You've gone to my head, like a strong wine, and I can't even think straight any more.' His breathing was ragged, and even beneath the thickness of their coats she could feel the heavy, pounding thud of his heartbeat. Her heart swelled with exultation. He wanted her. She recognised it and she clung to him, overwhelmed by the desperate, passionate desire he was evoking in her.

'I'm glad you came along,' she said huskily. 'I was feeling lost and alone, and now I feel as though everything's all right.'

'It will be, you'll see.'

The heady moment dissipated as the sound of a car's engine came closer, and they broke apart a little. Lucas kept his arm around her shoulders, keeping her close to his side, and they began to walk back towards the farmhouse.

They didn't speak for a while, and all Sophie could think about was his nearness, the warmth of his long body, the strength of the arms that drew her to him.

'How could you want to leave all this?' he said, breaking the silence as the ivy-covered building came into view. 'It's beautiful.'

She gazed up at the house. Snow covered the gabled roofs and sparkled in the cold daylight, while icicles hung down in glistening perfection from the eaves.

Lucas shook his head in disbelief. 'You surely can't be thinking of selling up. There are generations of history locked up in there.'

'But not my history,' she answered in a quiet voice.

His mouth flattened. 'You're letting your emotions run away with you. It's far too soon for you to be making a decision of such importance.'

'I don't see it that way. My parents deceived me. They kept me in the dark. I didn't even know that I've probably been suffering my whole life from a disease I doubtless inherited from my natural parents. If they'd told me, if they'd been straightforward with me, I might have found out much sooner, and maybe I could have done something about it earlier. That way, I perhaps wouldn't need to take a trip to the doctor's office every week for the next year...because that's what it will amount to if my GP's supposition is right.'

'Your parents loved you and brought you up as their own. They did everything they could to make you part of their lives and to ensure that you had a happy childhood. You can't think of throwing it away.'

She stiffened, moving away from him and starting to walk up the path to the house. 'You don't understand,' she said flatly. 'You just see me as female and emotional and you don't really know what I'm going through, what I'm feeling.' She looked at him. 'It doesn't matter. I can deal with this on my own. I *will* deal with it on my own.'

His mouth tightened. 'There you are...you're doing it again, aren't you? Shutting me out. How can I ever hope to get through to you if you keep doing that?'

She gave him a doleful stare. 'The answer's simple enough,' she said. 'Don't try. I'll be fine.'

CHAPTER SEVEN

'WOULD you like some help with that?'

Sophie finished fixing the red and gold garland in place above the nurses' station and then peered down at Lucas from her precarious position at the top of the stepladder. 'Thanks,' she said with a smile. 'I could definitely do with some help here. I'm really not good with heights, but the children have been so excited about the decorations ever since we put the tree up, and they'll be disappointed if I don't finish them this afternoon.'

'Hmm.' He looked her over, his gaze lingering on her smooth, shapely legs emerging from beneath the gently flowing fabric of her skirt. 'I thought you looked a bit unsteady up there. Here, let me give you a hand to get down.'

He reached for her, his hands going around her waist as she bent towards him, and in one strong, capable movement, he lifted her to the floor. Giving her a moment to steady herself, he kept his hands around her, and as their bodies meshed, Sophie felt a pool of heat flare in her abdomen. It spread out in ever-widening circles to light sparks throughout her body, making her conscious of each and every place where they touched, his thighs against hers, the wall of his chest lightly pressuring her breasts, his head bent towards her so that his mouth was just a breath away from hers.

Lucas was in no hurry to release her. Instead, his hands lightly stroked the small of her back and slid to the rounded swell of her hips.

A soft thud came from the nearest bay, as one of the children dropped a book, and Sophie made a desperate effort to recover herself. It wouldn't do for one of the nurses to come along and find her up close to him like this, would it?

'Um…are things a bit slow down in A and E?' she asked. 'How come you have time on your hands?' She tried not to think about what those hands were doing to her right now, his thumbs making slow circles on her hips and sending scorching messages to fire up needs she'd never even known she had. Gently, reluctantly, she tried to ease herself away from him.

A rueful smile touched his lips. He let go of her, and said, 'I'm on my lunch break. I dare say if things hot up, Debbie will page me, so in the meantime I'm all yours.' He sent her a devilish smile, his gaze resting on the ripe fullness of her mouth. 'You can take that any way you like.'

'You're a wicked man, Lucas Blake,' she answered huskily, 'saying such things in front of all these innocents.'

'Just as well they can't hear me, then,' he murmured, unabashed. 'But you're quite right. Wrong place, wrong time.'

He turned his attention to the Christmas decorations, walking over to where they were stored. Lifting out a garland, he held it up and asked, 'Where do you want this?'

'Wherever you think would be good. I'm expecting a new admission to the ward any time in the next half-hour, and I'd like to get this out of the way before she arrives.' She looked around. 'Maybe we could have one or two strung out on the walls between the windows in each bay and over the doorways.'

'Consider it done.' He opened up the garland, a stream of red and gold foil that glinted under the overhead lights. 'Who's your new admission? Has she been referred to you by her GP?'

'Actually, she's being transferred from a specialist centre at a London hospital. She had surgery there for biliary atresia, and now she's coming home for the recovery phase. From what I hear, the operation was successful, and they're hopeful her bile duct is working properly now.'

'How old is she? These things are much more successful if they're done while the child is very young.' He looked at her, his expression serious, and she nodded.

'You're right. She's just a baby—only six weeks old. Poor little thing, her bile ducts hadn't been draining properly since birth, so her jaundice was really bad, and of course it will take some time for that to clear.'

'I expect her parents will be glad to have her closer to home anyway.'

'Yes.' She taped a shiny silver snowflake onto the wall.

'So, have you gone ahead and put the farm on the market, as you said you would?' Lucas sent her an oblique glance.

She shook her head. 'Not yet. I thought about what you said and decided I should give it a bit longer. You were right, I was over-emotional, and that's no time to be making decisions.' She frowned. 'I still feel the same way about it, though.'

'You'll probably feel that way for some time. If I were you, I'd put it on hold for at least six months. That should give you a proper chance to sort yourself out. As it is, you've not been well, and that's another reason for delaying things.'

'Actually, I've been trying to follow a special diet, cutting out iron and vitamin C, fruit juices and so on, and generally I'm trying to eat healthily, making sure I'm getting all the right nutrients to compensate. I don't know whether I'm imagining it, but some of my aches and pains already seem to be less noticeable.'

She picked out a cheerful snowman, bright with

a long, red scarf around his neck and shiny buttons down his front, and placed him close by the snowflake.

He nodded. 'That's a good sign. But, as I said, you shouldn't rush things. Wait until you're feeling properly better before you make a move. You're angry with your parents right now, but maybe you should try to think about things from their viewpoint. They couldn't have children of their own, I imagine, and you would have been a joy to them.' He smiled. 'You're a joy to everyone who meets you…the children love you, and the staff always have good things to say about you. It seems to me that, no matter what you think now, your parents did a good job somewhere along the line.'

She chuckled. 'I get the feeling you're more than a little prejudiced,' she murmured. She added tinsel to the big Christmas tree that had pride of place by the nurses' station, where it could be seen by children from the bays all around.

Just as they were putting the last glittering lantern in place, Hannah came into the ward, accompanied by a specialist nurse wheeling a baby in a cot. 'Here she is, our baby Charlotte,' the specialist nurse said. 'Not a very happy little girl, at the moment, I'm afraid.'

The infant was crying, the fretful, insistent cry of a tiny child wanting attention.

Sophie went to greet the nurse, and Lucas followed. 'How is she doing, medically?'

'Not too bad at all, considering,' the nurse answered. 'Nothing untoward happened on the journey over here but, as you can hear, she's a bit out of sorts right now. I've changed her nappy, and she's had some formula, so it can't be either of those things causing the problem.' She handed Sophie a folder. 'These are her notes, and all the transfer forms.' She looked around, and said approvingly, 'It all looks very cheerful in here. You're certainly all prepared for Christmas.'

'We are…or at least, I hope we are.' Sophie leaned over the cot and tried to soothe the baby, talking to her softly and letting her curl her tiny fists around her finger.

She smiled at the nurse. 'We have a good cafeteria here, if you want to go and get yourself a drink and something to eat. You'll have some time to spare before you make the journey home, I expect?'

The nurse nodded. 'The paramedics are already down there,' she said. 'That's where I'll be, if you need me in the next half-hour or so.'

She left the ward a few minutes later, and Sophie and Lucas wheeled the child into a prepared space in the nearest bay, while Hannah went to check up on another patient.

Sophie gazed down at the baby, whose cries had turned into hiccupping sobs. 'Poor little mite, to have go through surgery at such a young age.' Very carefully, she lifted the infant from the cot and cradled her in her arms. 'What's wrong, little one?' she said softly. 'Are you missing your mum? She'll be along soon. I expect she's been held up in the traffic.'

'You must have the magic touch,' Lucas said, watching her as she rocked the baby gently. 'She's stopped crying.'

'I think she just wanted a cuddle,' Sophie murmured, smiling down at the gurgling infant. Little bubbles came from a rosebud mouth, and dimples appeared in her cheeks as she started to coo. Sophie held the warm little bundle against her breast, loving the feel of this tiny child nestling against her. Had her own natural parents felt this way when they'd held her in their arms for the first time?

Misty-eyed, she stroked the baby's soft skin and thought about the babies she might have some day. She would never be able to part with them, she felt sure. What could have happened to make her natural parents put her up for adoption?

Lucas laid the palm of his hand on the small of her back. 'You look sad,' he murmured. 'Are you thinking about your biological parents?'

She nodded. She might have known he would be in tune with her thoughts. He had always been able to read her. It was like an instinct with him. He had a mysterious ability to fathom each and every one of her warring emotions.

'There's only one way you're going to be able to resolve that issue,' he said. 'Perhaps you should go back to the adoption agency, and see if they can help you to find them.'

She nodded. 'Things should be easier these days, shouldn't they? Everything is usually documented, and if the agency does manage to find my parents, I could try to get in touch.' She frowned. 'That's if they want to hear from me. I suppose they could refuse. Not everyone wants to meet up with their offspring years later, when their families are established. It could cause all kinds of problems for them.'

'Now you're running way ahead of yourself again,' Lucas warned. 'Let's deal with one thing at a time.' He looked at the baby, who was staring contentedly up at her from the safe haven of her arms. 'It looks as though she's going to be your priority for the next hour or so.' He smiled. 'I'd better go back down to A and E and leave you to it. Will I see you at the Christmas party tonight?'

She blinked. 'Is it tonight? Heavens, that came around quickly.' The party was being held at the hospital, in one of the lecture halls that would have been trimmed for the occasion and decked out with tables and chairs around a large dance area. 'Hannah's been talking about it, trying to persuade me to go, but I'm not sure. I don't feel as though I'm ready to celebrate anything.'

'All the more reason for you to come along,' he

said. 'Come with me, and forget your troubles for a while. I'll pick you up around eight o'clock.'

'I don't know. I ought to stay at the farm and keep an eye on the animals.' She tried to stall him. 'Jessie's not herself, the hens aren't laying nearly as many eggs as usual, and Ferdie's gone into a kind of depression. He's just not the bossy goose he once was.' She frowned. 'Besides, I doubt I'd be very good company. I really don't think…'

'None of those excuses is of any major, earth-shattering importance. You're letting your problems get the better of you, and you need a break. Like I said, I'll be at the farmhouse at eight, and if you're not ready, I'll wait until you are.'

'You do realise that's out-and-out harassment, don't you?' she said in mild protest.

'Yeah.' He grinned. 'I'll see you later.'

Sophie pulled a face and looked down at little Charlotte once more. She'd fallen asleep and looked to have hardly a care in the world. Sophie smiled. Somehow she couldn't avoid being drawn into the festive celebrations. They were descending on her like an unstoppable juggernaut. Decorating the wards was just a start.

She'd arranged for Santa to come in and visit the children who were unfortunate enough to be in hospital at this time of year, and she'd spent an hour or two wrapping presents for him to give out. Next week there would be Christmas dinner in the cafeteria, and now the party loomed. Most of the staff who weren't on duty would be there and everyone would think it odd if she didn't attend. They wouldn't understand her reluctance. They revelled in the chance to let their hair down and forget about work for a while, and they would all be looking forward to the countdown to Christmas.

After placing her back in her cot, she checked Charlotte's medication. She was on antibiotics, to prevent infection of the bile ducts that might be a complication after the surgery, and those would continue for some time to come. Then there were drugs to prevent the build-up of fluid in her abdomen and alongside that she would be given nutritional supplements.

'You're doing well, precious,' she murmured,

looking down at the sleeping infant. Once the jaundice cleared, evidence that the bile ducts were working properly, she would be well and truly on the mend.

She made a final round of the ward, stopping for a cheery word with all those children who were up for it and spending time with those who were still too poorly to respond with much enthusiasm. She cared for each and every one of them, and she knew that with time and good nursing each one would make a full recovery. That was what made her job worthwhile.

The end of her shift came, and Sophie set off for home. Without a doubt, Lucas would turn up on her doorstep at eight, and she was equally certain that he'd meant it when he'd said he would wait until she was ready—there was no way he would let her skip out of this one.

She opened the doors to her wardrobe and looked inside, searching for inspiration. What should she wear? Christmas parties were glitzy occasions and all the girls would be looking glamorous and ready for action. She had to find something dressy.

She dithered for half an hour, and then went to shower. The warm water would be refreshing and it might help to clear her head. Maybe it would wash away the cares of the day and leave her feeling invigorated.

The doorbell rang as she was putting the finishing touches to her make-up. She took a last, quick look in the mirror and then hurried downstairs. What would Lucas think of the way she looked? Would he like the way she'd done her hair, gathered up into a loose, flyaway topknot with tendrils that looped and curled in various directions?

'Come in,' she said, opening the door to him. 'You're early.' She stood to one side to let him in, but he stayed where he was, unmoving.

His eyes widened, an arrested look coming into them, his mouth slightly open on a swift intake of breath. 'You look…sensational,' he said at last. 'Absolutely stunning.'

'Um…I'm glad you think so.' She wasn't sure quite what she'd expected, but it was nothing like this. He still hadn't moved, and it was as though he couldn't take his eyes off her.

His gaze trailed over the shining honey gold of her hair, and lingered for a moment on the creamy, bare slopes of her shoulders. She felt the heat of it as his glance wandered over the smooth lines of her party frock, a figure-hugging creation of blush-pink silk, decorated at the breast with a smattering of crystal.

'Are you coming in?' she murmured. 'It's cold out there, but there's a log fire burning in the grate in the living room, and I think we might have time for a glass of something to warm us up before we set off.'

She watched as he visibly tried to pull himself together. 'Believe me, I'm already burning up,' he said in a husky voice, flame leaping in the depths of his grey eyes. 'You always look good, but tonight you're fabulous.'

He stepped into the hallway, and closed the door behind him, following Sophie into the living room. She was walking on air. Sensational, he'd said…stunning. It was much, much more than she might ever have hoped for and her confidence soared.

She went over to the drinks cabinet and started

to mix a couple of martinis. 'Are you okay to drink?' she asked.

He nodded. 'Just the one for now. I'll leave the car at the hospital and order a taxi for us later on.' He accepted the drink, and lifted his glass to her, toasting her with appreciative grey eyes.

The fire in the grate crackled, orange flames casting a warm glow over the wood panelling, while golden light from the lamps highlighted polished wood and threw shadows on the glass-fronted bookcases and lit up brass plates on the walls.

Sophie returned his gaze. 'You look pretty good yourself,' she murmured. There was something about the way he wore a suit. It made him stand out among men, the fine fabric and flawless lines complementing his broad shoulders and lean, flat-stomached perfection. And yet he was so easy within himself, wearing it as though he was in his natural element.

He smiled. 'I'm glad you decided to come to the party,' he said. 'I'm sure you'll have a good time once we get there.'

'Hmm. I remember the last party I went to didn't turn out so well.'

He raised a dark brow. 'The wedding, you mean?'

She nodded. 'I made a fool of myself, fainting.'

He shrugged. 'I don't recall too much about that. All I know is that you knocked me out. You were so beautiful. I felt as though I'd stumbled on heaven and I was worried in case I woke up and found I'd been dreaming.'

She laughed. 'You have such a silver tongue. No wonder you get on so well with all the female staff at the hospital. They're all desperate for so much as a look, or even a nod from you.'

'Nah.' He dismissed her suggestion with a crooked smile. 'You're imagining things.'

She didn't think she was. He was hot property, and maybe she ought to be glad that he was paying her so much attention. Even now, she couldn't imagine why he was so taken with her, offering his support at every turn, but perhaps that might be because she was the one woman who persistently refused to be swayed by his advances. That would be unfamiliar territory to

Lucas and perhaps, unwittingly, she had become a challenge to him.

He glanced at his watch. 'I think it's time we were setting off,' he said, putting his empty glass down on a table. He laid a hand gently beneath her elbow. 'Let me take you to the ball, Cinders. Your carriage awaits.'

She chuckled, and went with him. For that moment in time she really did feel as though she had found her prince.

As soon as they arrived at the hall, the party atmosphere enveloped them. The lighting was subdued, a band was playing and Sophie could see her friends moving to the music on the polished floor. Hannah waved and she smiled and waved back in return.

'I'll get you a drink,' Lucas suggested. 'Something hot and sultry to reflect the way you look.'

She smiled in acknowledgment. She felt better already. The night was young and full of promise, and she was with the one man who could make her pulse race and her heart sing.

They joined their friends on the dance floor, and Sophie lost herself for a while in the rhythm of the music and the sheer enjoyment of being with Lucas. He was good fun, energetic, and he moved with her in time with the beat as though he was born to it.

They took a well-earned rest after a while, moving to the side of the room, where they helped themselves to food from the buffet table. Hannah and her boyfriend, a medical student in his registration year, came to join them.

They ate for a while, chatting about this and that, and then Lucas went to fetch drinks.

'I feel I ought to be toasting you with champagne,' he said, coming back and handing her the white wine spritzer she'd asked for. 'You're sparkling tonight. White wine doesn't do you justice.'

'I like it,' she murmured, sipping her drink and enjoying the mix of wine and soda. 'I'm glad you bullied me into coming.'

'Persuaded,' he murmured, cutting in. 'Persuaded is the word.' He lifted a dark brow. 'Would I do anything so crass as to bully you?'

She laughed. 'Perhaps not...but I'm having a great time, all the same. You were right. I needed a break.' Being with him was good, too...extra-specially good. It was as though she had been going through life in a fog, these last few months. She had seen Lucas, and yet she had not seen him. He had been there for her the whole time, but she had been too wrapped up in her problems to appreciate everything that he was.

'You have that dazed look in your eyes again,' he said softly. 'Where have you gone to? What are you thinking?'

She took another sip of her drink. 'I was just thinking what a great atmosphere there is in here,' she murmured, looking around. 'I feel sorry for those people who will miss out because they have to be on duty at the hospital.'

'Some will still be able to make it, depending on shift changes.'

Hannah came alongside them and helped herself to salted nuts. 'Debbie was one of the unlucky ones, wasn't she? I know she was hoping to be here.'

Lucas frowned. 'That's true. A last-minute shift change meant she has to work through the night. I know she hates doing that, because she has to spread herself thinly between the wards and A and E.'

Sophie frowned. 'That's tough, isn't it?' she commented. 'It's a raw deal either way.' She sent him a cautious glance. 'You and she have been working together quite closely, haven't you?'

Lucas nodded, and Hannah put in quietly, 'I think she looks to you for guidance.'

'I suppose she does.' His expression was sombre for a moment or two. 'It's not easy for junior doctors, and she seemed particularly vulnerable when I started here, so I suppose we gravitated towards one another.'

He looked at Sophie's empty glass. 'Do you want another, or shall we go and join the others on the dance floor?'

He was changing the subject, and after a moment's hesitation Sophie took the hint and didn't pursue it any further. She didn't want to spoil the evening. He wasn't with Debbie now, he was with her, so she put down her glass and said brightly, 'I'm up for dancing, if you are?'

Towards the end of the evening, as more and more drinks had flowed, and people were slipping into a mellow mood, the band began to play gentler, more romantic tunes.

Lucas held her close, so that they swayed together, his cheek resting against hers, his thighs lightly nudging her legs. She was happy, glad to be with him, and she wished that the evening didn't have to end.

As they returned to their table some time later for a breather, she was aware of a soft, trilling sound interspersed with the low buzz of conversation all around.

'Is that your phone?' Hannah asked, looking to where Sophie had placed her handbag.

Sophie nodded, reaching for her phone while Hannah and her boyfriend went back onto the dance floor as the band struck up a lilting melody. It was a bit late for anyone to be phoning her, wasn't it? She checked the caller's name, and frowned.

Nathan. What could he want at this hour?

'Sorry it's so late,' Nathan said quickly, forestalling her, 'but I've been out on call to a farm not too far away from yours. I stopped by your place on the way home, but of course you weren't there.'

'I'd forgotten you work unsocial hours,' she said. 'I'm at a Christmas party. You can probably hear the noise in the background.'

'Yes.' She heard the smile in his voice. 'I wish I could be there with you.'

She remained silent, and after a second or two of hesitation he added, 'Anyway, you said you've been having a few problems with the animals, so I thought I'd stop by and take a look at them. Of course, I discovered that everywhere's locked up tonight, so I had to leave it. Maybe I could come over tomorrow it's your half-day then, isn't it?'

'Yes, that would be fine. I'll see you then.'

She finished the call and placed the phone back in her bag. She was pensive for a while. It still seemed a little odd that he had rung her so late, despite what he had said. Was he still hankering after renewing their relationship?

She looked up to see that Lucas was watching her intently. A deep line had etched itself into his brow, and she guessed he had found it easy enough to work out who had called her.

'It was Nathan,' she said, all the same, wanting to show that she was being open with him. 'He's going to take a look at the animals for me.'

'I gathered it was him,' Lucas answered, an edge of cynicism coming into his voice. 'I expect he'll do a good job. After all, he must be very keen, if he's calling you at this hour. How many other vets would go to so much trouble?'

'You have to give him some leeway,' Sophie murmured, disturbed by the tension she saw in his features. His grey eyes held a chilling expression and his jaw was rigid, a taut muscle flicking there. 'He's finding it hard to let go.'

'And you're not making it any easier for him, are you?'

'I'm doing the best I can. It's a difficult situation.'

'Yeah, sure it is.'

Sophie frowned, stung by his implied criticism of her. 'I don't see why you're having such a problem with it,' she said, her tone blunt. 'What is it that's going on here? Why are you so concerned about it? Are we colleagues, friends, or is it something more than that? And if that's the case, you can hardly argue you've been keeping yourself to yourself, can you? It doesn't seem to bother you overmuch when the nurses make eyes at you…and what's with Debbie and all those evenings you've spent together? I don't see how you can complain—it isn't as though we've made some sort of commitment to one another, is it?'

His eyes narrowed on her. 'Does that bother you—the time I've spent with Debbie?'

She pulled in a sharp breath. 'I didn't say that,' she said, suddenly conscious that he'd managed to call her bluff. 'I'm just pointing out that you're in no position to complain.'

'Hey, you two…' Hannah came over to their table and cut in on their heated discussion. 'They're drawing the raffle. You need to have your tickets handy.'

'Oh… Yes… I'll find them.' Flustered, Sophie acknowledged the nurse. Hannah and her boyfriend sat down at the table, and any chance of finishing the conversation with Lucas was gone.

The phone call had put an end to everything.

The evening was ruined, the happy party atmosphere had been banished, and she had no idea how to go about putting things right.

CHAPTER EIGHT

'DID you get caught up in the storm last night?' Hannah wanted to know as Sophie came on to the children's ward to start her rounds. 'According to the news reports, it caused all kinds of damage.'

'No.' Sophie shook her head. 'Luckily I was home before it began, but I heard it banging away in the early hours of the morning. The wind was so bad it broke down one of the fences on the farm. I still haven't had time to take a proper look to see if it caused any other damage.'

'Oh, dear. You could do without that.'

'Yes.' In truth, though, it felt as though the real storm had been going on inside her, and this morning she was a total wreck. Lucas had dropped her off at home last night, and nothing had been resolved between them. He had been distant with her, and the bond between them was broken. She felt empty, as though she had lost something precious.

'Young Marcus is back for his heart surgery,' Hannah reminded her, going through the list of admissions. 'Mr Burnley's scheduled the operation for early this morning.'

'That's good.' With any luck, the child should be back from Theatre before she had to go off duty this afternoon. 'We'll need to get him prepped and make sure his parents are calm and that they understand everything that's happening. We have to help them so that they can keep up a lot of positive vibes around Marcus.'

'I'll spend all the time I can with them,' Hannah said, nodding. 'They've been very good with him up to now, but of course it's always traumatic when a child has major surgery. It's bound to be upsetting.'

'That's true. It must be awful to know that your child has been born with an illness—there must always be the question at the back of your mind as to whether or not it was your fault…if it was something you did or didn't do while you were pregnant that caused the problem.'

She frowned, thinking about that. How would she respond if her child was ill? A feeling of dread crept over her. It wasn't just an idle question, was it? There was a distinct possibility that her children could inherit the disease that she had, or at least be carriers. Could she bring them into the world knowing that they, or their offspring, might suffer later in life?

She came back to the present with a start as the sound of a Christmas carol invaded her thoughts. Hannah had switched on the CD player, and music played softly in the background.

'There's not long to go now before the big day,' the nurse said with a smile. 'We might as well make the most of it and get the atmosphere right… And this the day when Santa's coming to visit the wards, isn't it?'

'Yes, you're right. Who's doing it this year? Dr Friedman always stepped in for us, but now he's in the States we're left with a bit of a problem.'

'Debbie told me Lucas was doing it. He was scheduled for teaching time today, but that's been cancelled, so apparently he's stepping into the breach.' Hannah's mouth curved. 'I think he'll be a great Santa. He's wonderful with the children. Whenever he comes on to the ward he tells them stories and makes them giggle. I just can't wait to see him in his outfit.'

He was good in every way, Sophie reflected, with adults and children alike. He had a perfect smile, a way of making you feel good about yourself. He was the kind of man you could easily fall for, a man you could easily love.

Her thoughts lingered there for a while, and it was as though something tilted and crashed inside her chest, knocking the breath out of her. Why hadn't she seen it before? Wasn't that the reason she felt so bad now that there was this gulf between them? She missed him, she needed him and the reason for that had only just dawned on her...she had fallen in love with him.

'At least he'll be here before Marcus goes to Theatre,' Hannah murmured, oblivious to Sophie's inner torment. 'He said he would start early so that Marcus could have his gift before he goes to Theatre. The excitement should help the lad to forget about the operation for a while.'

Sophie blinked and tried to follow what Hannah

was saying. She nodded. 'I'll go and see Marcus now,' she said, her voice thickening, 'before I do the rest of my rounds.'

The four-year-old was looking at a picture book with his mother when Sophie approached his bedside. He looked up, and said brightly, 'Look, Sophie, there's a house with twinkly lights, and it's snowing.' He pointed to the page, where golden light shone from the windows of a snow-covered house.

Sophie looked at the book. 'Ah, I see—if you go through the door, you'll find out what's inside the house.'

Marcus's eyes widened, and he carefully lifted the front door flap, to reveal a Christmas tree. 'Ahh…it's full of pretty baubles.' He looked at his mother. 'Have we got a tree like that at home?'

His mother nodded. 'We're going to put it up tomorrow, so that we'll be all ready for Christmas.'

Marcus frowned. 'Will I be able to see it?'

His mother nodded. 'Of course.' She turned and looked towards her husband, but only he and Sophie could see the fleeting anxiety in her eyes.

'When you've had your operation,' Sophie said, 'and you're feeling better, you'll be able to see all the decorations at home, and you'll be able to play without getting breathless. You shouldn't get those pains in your legs any more either.'

Marcus gave her a beaming smile. 'I'm having my operation today,' he said. 'I'm a little bit frightened, but Mummy says she'll stay with me until I go to sleep.'

'That's right. You don't have to worry about anything, because you'll be asleep through it all, and Mummy and Daddy will be waiting for you when you wake up.' Sophie checked his blood pressure and all the readings on the monitors. Everything seemed to be fine. 'I'll leave you to finish your book,' she said, 'and I'll be back in a while to give you your medicine. It should make you feel a bit sleepy.'

She was leaving the pre-med for as long as possible, in order to give Lucas a chance to do his Santa impersonation. She checked her watch. As long as he arrived in the next few minutes, all would be well.

'Ho, ho, ho...has anyone seen my reindeer?'

A big, bright, bustling Santa strode onto the ward, looking all around him. 'Has anyone seen Rudolph? He was with me a minute ago, but now I can't find him anywhere.' He scratched his silky white head and stroked his long beard, looking bemused. He went over to Marcus. 'Hello, little boy. Have you seen Rudolf? Has he been in here?'

Marcus solemnly shook his head. 'How will you get round without him?' he said, looking worried. 'He has to help you with the toys, doesn't he?'

Santa nodded. 'He does, but I expect he's gone for a wander. He's always looking for carrots, you know?'

'Is he?' Marcus's eyes were large, taking everything in.

'He is.' Lucas searched in his pockets and triumphantly brought out a couple of carrots. He showed them to all the children in the bay. 'Now, I wonder if I can tempt him back with these? Just you youngsters hang on here for a minute, and I'll go and see if I can find him.' He left the ward, and after a second or two they heard the jingle of bells coming from the corridor outside.

Sophie looked at the children. 'Do you know what that sounded like to me?' she asked.

The children shook their heads, and then one bright young spark said, 'I think it was Santa's sleigh.'

'I think you're right,' Sophie murmured. 'I bet you he's found Rudolph. But we'll soon see. He'll be back in a minute.'

Sure enough, Santa came back onto the ward, smiling broadly. He looked around. 'Never could resist a carrot, my Rudolph. He's promised me he'll stay there and keep all the other reindeer in order until I've given out all the toys to you boys and girls.'

A whisper of excitement went around the room as he produced a brightly coloured sack full of packages. 'Here we are, then. Let's see what we have for you.'

Marcus opened his present and showed it to his parents. 'I got a magic painting book and some coloured pencils,' he said, looking pleased. 'There's a paintbrush as well.'

'So all you need is a drop of water to brush across the picture, and then you can see what colours come out. Why don't you do the first one now? I expect Mummy can find you a little bit of water.' Sophie smiled at him and handed him a small plastic cup of liquid. 'This is your medicine,' she told him. 'Drink up.' The pre-med would make him drowsy before he went for his operation, and hopefully it would begin to work by the time he had finished his painting.

She went to see how Lucas was getting on. By now, he had finished giving out all the presents in his sack, and he had stopped to talk to Hannah.

Sophie approached him cautiously, uncertain what his reaction to her might be. She smiled at him and he nodded in her direction, but there was no answering smile, and his grey eyes didn't have their customary warmth. Instead his expression was remote, replaced after a while with professional courtesy.

'I think that went well enough, don't you?' he said.

'More than well. The children were thrilled to bits.' Sophie longed for him to give some small sign that he cared about her, but there was nothing. He believed she was still seeing Nathan, and it disturbed him so much that he was easing himself back from her, leaving the field open for her to go back to her ex. How could he do that if he truly wanted her, as he'd said?

But, then, she'd hardly given him the encouragement he deserved, had she? This was all her own fault. It had taken her too long to come to the realisation that he was the man she really loved.

Hannah went to check on Marcus, leaving Sophie alone with him. Sophie watched her go and then said softly, 'I'm sorry that last night turned out the way it did. We were having such a good time and I loved being with you. I wasn't expecting Nathan to call.'

He didn't answer, and she went on, 'He really does have to see to the animals—that's why he's coming to the farm this afternoon.'

He gave her a sceptical look. 'He's coming to see you. He thinks there's still a chance for him, and the only reason he'll think that way is because you've led him to believe it can happen.'

'I'm not encouraging him. I've told him that it's over, more than once, but he doesn't seem to be getting the message.'

He gave a light shrug. 'Perhaps your actions contradict your words.'

Sophie straightened her shoulders. 'I've told you the way things are,' she said. 'I can't do any more. I'm sorry you feel that way.' She shook her head as though to shake herself free of the troubles that were crowding in on her. No matter what she said, there was no way of getting through to him, and she was wasting her breath. 'I have to go and prepare Marcus for his operation. Perhaps I'll see you later.'

He nodded, and watched her walk away. She didn't see him leave the ward. She didn't look back. Instead, she put all her efforts into making sure that Marcus was ready for his operation, and that his parents were as prepared for it as they could be. It was a tense, anxious time for all of them.

When Marcus was finally wheeled into the operating theatre, Hannah showed his parents into the waiting room and brought them coffee and talked to them for a while. They were both upset.

Sophie tended to the rest of the children on the ward, making sure that their needs were taken care of, that they were comfortable and free from pain. After an hour or so, at lunchtime, there was still no news from Theatre, and she made her way to the hospital restaurant. She was hoping that Lucas might be there, but he was nowhere to be seen.

They were serving Christmas dinner. It was a full offering of turkey with all the trimmings, roast potatoes, new potatoes, sage and onion stuffing and a selection of winter vegetables. Sophie collected her tray and took it over to a table by the window. Outside, the wind was causing the branches of the trees to sway, and the sky was grey, heavy with perhaps with the promise of a fresh onset of snow.

She looked up as Debbie came to her table. 'Is it okay if I join you?' Debbie asked. She looked weary.

'Of course. Sit down,' Sophie murmured. 'I'm surprised that you're still on duty. I heard you were working the late shift last night.'

'I did. I've only just come on duty again. I've been home, but to be honest I didn't get much rest. I've been studying for exams, and it's taking its toll on me, I guess.'

'Lucas mentioned a while ago that you had some specialist exams coming up.'

Debbie nodded. 'He's been helping me. He's been more than good to me, really, coming round to the house, going over old exam papers with me, showing me the areas I needed to concentrate on.' She gave a wan smile. 'He's worked so hard with me, I don't know what he'll say if I don't pass this exam.'

So that's what Lucas had been doing when he spent time with Debbie. Sophie's heart sank. Why hadn't she trusted him? Lucas had never put a foot wrong and she should never have doubted him.

'I expect he'll say that you did your best, whatever happens,' she said. 'Anyway, I'm sure you'll do well. You always put in a good effort, whatever you're doing. The main thing is, you need to try to get some rest. No one can think properly when they haven't had enough sleep. Believe me, I know what I'm saying.'

Debbie nodded. 'That's what my fiancé keeps

telling me. "Get some rest and you'll be fine."' She smiled. 'We're planning on getting married as soon as my exams are over and done with. I can't wait.'

'That's wonderful,' Sophie said with a smile. 'Congratulations.'

They chatted for a while, then finished their meals and went their separate ways. Sophie went back to the ward in time to learn that Marcus had been taken from Theatre and the recovery room straight to Intensive Care. She went over there to see him, and to talk to his parents.

'He'll be sedated for a while,' she said, 'but Mr Burnley told me that the surgery went well. He'll be along to see you just as soon as he's free.' She looked at Marcus, sleeping peacefully in the bed, with tubes coming from various parts of his body and leads attaching him to monitors. It was a frightening sight for any parent to see. 'If all goes well, he'll be in hospital for just over a week—which means that there's a chance he might be home with you for Christmas.'

His mother gave a relieved smile. 'Thank you for coming to talk to us. You've all been so friendly and helpful. I don't think we could have gone through this otherwise.'

'You're welcome. Stay with him, if you like, though I expect he'll sleep for quite some time. Perhaps you would like a hot drink or something to eat? If you don't want to go along to the restaurant, there are a couple of machines outside in the corridor and another one in the waiting room round the corner.'

'Thanks.'

Sophie left them to watch their son and decided it was time for her to go home. First thing this morning she'd carried out a makeshift repair to the fence back at the farm, and she was anxious to know whether it was still holding. The wind had died down a bit during the course of the morning, but it was bitterly cold, with the ever-present threat of more snow, and she wasn't looking forward to doing more repairs.

When she arrived back at the house, though, things were much worse than she could have imagined. Her hastily erected fence panel and wooden brace hadn't lasted the course, and now George, the goat, was off in the vegetable patch, eating whatever he happened upon. Ferdie fluffed out his feathers and joined him, hopping disconsolately over the windswept garden. She looked in consternation at half-eaten winter cabbages and broccoli stems that were broken and battered.

'That's it, George,' she said sternly. She wasn't too concerned about the goose. He would follow wherever she went. 'You've had all the freedom you're going to get for today.' Putting up a determined effort, she chased the goat around the vegetable garden and went after him when he jumped over the fence and into the meadow. It took a good twenty minutes of patient manoeuvring and attempts to outwit him before she managed to grab hold of him and tether him with a long rope to a fence in the courtyard. Honeysuckle and Daisy watched her efforts with interest from the safety of the paddock, and she frowned in their direction. 'Don't go getting any ideas,' she told the Shetlands. 'I'm really not in the mood.'

She went inside the house and spent some half an hour on the phone, ringing round to find someone who could come and fix the fence for her, but it appeared that everyone she spoke to was too busy until after Christmas.

She drummed her fingers on the kitchen table for a while and then in desperation she phoned Lucas.

He was at home, from what she could gather, and she heard sounds of children's voices in the background.

'I'm sorry,' she said. 'I didn't realise that you had the children with you. I didn't mean to disturb you.'

'You're not disturbing me. Ella's back in hospital, Tom's away again, and I have them until my parents get back from choosing a Christmas tree from the local forest.' His tone was brisk and to the point. 'What was it that you wanted?'

'Um...' She put her worries to one side for the moment, alarmed to hear that his sister was having problems. 'Is Ella ill again? Is her blood pressure high?'

'It spiked a little. The children are off school for the Christmas holidays, and I suspect she hasn't had time to rest. The midwife visited her this morning and had her admitted as a precaution since she's not too far off her delivery date. We've called Tom to let him know, but my parents were already out when it happened.' He paused. 'What was it that you were ringing me about?'

She hesitated. Maybe she had done the wrong thing in calling him. He didn't sound pleased to hear from her. He wasn't giving away any of his thoughts.

'I was hoping for some advice, really. You see, one of the fences blew down this morning, and I tried to fix it temporarily by wedging a couple of posts up against it and nailing a few planks crosswise here and there, but when I arrived home, I found it had blown down again. I've been through the phone book but I can't find anyone who will come out and mend it for me, and I'm not quite sure how to go about things. I thought a couple of posts would do the trick, but obviously the weight was too much for them, with the wind still blowing, and for some reason the planks I nailed up have come down as well.'

'Did you make a hole in the ground to stand the posts in?'

She frowned. 'No. Should I have done that?'

'Well, it helps to stabilise things. What about the nails you used? What size were they?'

'Um… I don't know really. I just grabbed what was to hand—they were about the size of a fingernail, perhaps.'

'Hmm. Most likely they're too short.'

'Oh, I see.' She was deflated for a moment or two. All her efforts at being independent had been useless. 'I'll go down to the hardware shop in the village, then. I expect they'll have what I need.' She hesitated. 'Thanks, Lucas. I'll have a go at digging a few holes and see if I can brace things a bit better.'

'No, don't do that. Leave it. I'll come and take a look at it for you.'

'No…no, I can't burden you with my troubles when you already have enough on your plate. I'll sort it out, don't worry about me.'

'I'll be there in half an hour,' he said, his tone still brisk. 'It means you'll have William and Emily for company, though. I hope that's not going to be a problem?'

'Of course it won't. I like having them here—but you really don't have to go to all that trouble.

All I needed was some advice, and you've given it to me.'

'Just leave the fence to me,' he said, and cut the call.

Sophie stared at the phone for a minute or two after he had rung off. He'd sounded abrupt for the most part, and she didn't know what to make of his mood. She so wanted things to be right between them, but there was no knowing what was going on in his head.

He'd said he was coming to help out, though, and her spirits lifted at that. It didn't mean that he thought any differently about the situation between them—after all, he would do the same for any one in need, just as he had helped Debbie. But at least it was a start. He was coming over to the farm and she had to be glad about that.

'Hello, Sophie,' William greeted her, arriving with a clatter a short time later. He was helping to carry some of the tools that Lucas had brought with him—Sophie suspected that he'd badgered his uncle to be allowed to help. 'My mummy's in hospital again.' His expression was serious.

'I heard about that,' Sophie said. 'I'm sorry...

that must be upsetting for you.' She glanced at Emily to include her in what she was saying. 'But I'm sure she'll be all right. The doctors and nurses will all look after her.'

Emily nodded solemnly. 'She's going to have the baby soon,' she said. 'I don't know if I'm going to have a little brother or sister, but…' She paused to look thoughtfully at William, and then went on, 'I think I'd actually like a sister.'

William didn't appear to be put out by that. His mind was on other things. 'We have to mend the fence,' he told Sophie. 'It's men's work.' He puffed out his chest. This was important business.

Lucas sent him an amused look and then turned his attention to Sophie. 'If you want to show me where this fence is, I'll make a start.' He looked at William. 'Correction, we'll make a start.'

'Thanks. I'll give you a hand.'

'That won't be necessary. I can manage.'

'Oh, okay.' She was a little taken aback by his abrupt manner, but she didn't say any more and led them outside, beyond the paddock where Honeysuckle and Daisy stood by the fence, curious to see what was going on. Their ears pricked up when they saw the children, and Honeysuckle gave a low whinny of greeting.

'Will we be able to ride the ponies today?' Emily asked in a low voice.

Sophie nodded. 'Of course. We'll get kitted up in a few minutes if you like while Lucas works on the fence.' She glanced at William. 'As soon as you've finished helping, you can have a ride, too.'

'Yes, please,' William said, his eyes sparkling.

She showed Lucas the fallen fence, and he quickly sized up the situation. 'These things are heavy,' he commented. 'I'm surprised you managed to get it up in the first place. Leave it with me. I should be able to fix it so that it's as good as new.' He placed his toolbox on the ground beside him and opened it up. It looked to Sophie as though he had everything he needed, even a good selection of nails.

'You seem to be well prepared,' she murmured. 'Are you used to doing this sort of thing?'

'I help out quite a bit on my parents' farm. There are always jobs to be done and I quite like doing it. It makes a big change from medicine, and I enjoy doing physical work and being out in the open air.' He looked up at the sky. 'I'm not so sure about days like these, though,' he added with a frown. 'I wouldn't be surprised if it starts to snow any time now.'

She would have answered him, but there was the sound of a car drawing up in the courtyard by the stables, and she looked over there to see that Nathan had arrived. By her side, Lucas stiffened.

Nathan climbed out of the car and came towards them. 'Hi, Sophie.' He nodded towards Lucas and the children, who were watching this new visitor with interest. 'How are you doing?'

'Fine,' she said, 'except for a little trouble with the fence. Lucas is going to do what he can to fix it for me.'

She was surprised, and at the same time filled with a sudden surge of happiness, when Lucas slid a possessive arm around her waist. His gaze met Nathan's, and there was a clear understanding between the two men. *She's mine. Hands off.* Lucas's gesture left no room for doubt, either in

Nathan's mind or Sophie's. She dragged air into her lungs in an effort to calm herself.

His palm was warm against her rib cage. Even though she was wearing a cashmere sweater over her jeans, and a windcheater to keep out the cold, she could feel the sure strength of his arm about her. Her heart seemed to swell inside her chest. He still cared. He was prepared to make a stand for her.

Nathan braced himself. 'You said you were having problems with some of the animals,' he said.

'Yes.' She glanced up at Lucas and made to ease herself away from him. He let her go and she faltered momentarily, saddened by the loss of his strong, protective presence. 'It's Jessie I'm concerned about most of all…all she does is eat and she's putting on a lot of weight. And Ferdie's moping. He was always full of himself before, but now he's a shadow of what he used to be.'

Nathan nodded. 'And you say the hens aren't laying too well?'

'That's right. Egg production's right down—I

don't mind about that, but I just wonder if something's wrong with them.'

Nathan nodded. 'I'll take a look at them.'

'I'll come with you.' Sophie made to follow him, but Nathan stopped her.

'It's all right. I'll be fine on my own.' He looked at Emily. 'Besides, I think you have other things to do right now.'

'All right, if you're sure.' She waited as he walked away, and then turned to Lucas, wanting to be close to him, her confidence growing after his show of possessiveness. She wasn't sure what she was going to say to him, but she had to do something.

Lucas, though, was already busy working on the fence. He had anchored a post into the ground to keep it from falling, and now he was busy with hammer and nails. William was handing the nails to him as they were needed, and after Lucas finished putting each one in place, William finished things off, using his own small hammer.

Sophie watched Lucas as he worked, her gaze fixed on his strong, muscular body. She was fascinated by the way he moved with smooth precision to drive his target home each time, his body and his actions perfectly synchronised.

She backed slowly away from him. She was dizzy with a sudden, aching need that could not be fulfilled. She wanted to feel those strong arms around her, she longed for his kisses, and most of all she wanted to feel safe and secure in knowing that he was an integral part of her world. Would that ever come about? Her stomach twisted with uncertainty.

She went to find Emily, who was over by the paddock, stroking the Shetland ponies, each in turn. 'Let's go and saddle up Daisy, shall we?' she said, glancing at the little girl. 'You've been very patient.'

A few minutes later, she lightly held the lead rein as Emily sat on the Shetland pony and walked the horse around the meadow. Emily laughed as Daisy threw back her head in sheer enjoyment. 'I think she likes me.' She chuckled.

'She does. The ponies look forward to seeing you and William. They know they're going to get a lot of fuss and maybe a treat.'

By the time they'd finished a circuit of the

meadow, William was ready and waiting for his turn. Sophie saddled up Honeysuckle and led the two ponies out side by side. 'They like being together,' she told the children.

'But Daisy's jealous of Honeysuckle,' Emily said with a laugh. 'She tried to nudge Honeysuckle out of the way when I gave her an apple. She didn't want him to get it.'

'That's true. But Honeysuckle can act the same way sometimes. It's because they both want your attention.'

They finished riding in a while, and slid down from the saddles. 'Perhaps you should go and see if Lucas needs any more help,' Sophie murmured, 'while I see to the ponies.'

They hurried away in search of their uncle, and Sophie set about grooming the Shetlands and settling them back in the paddock with a feed of hay. If the weather proved too cold for them, they could wander into the stable block for shelter.

'I've finished looking at the animals,' Nathan said, coming into the shed where she was hanging up the harnesses.

She turned to look at him. 'Is it anything bad?' she asked. 'Anything I've been doing wrong?'

'No, nothing like that.' His gaze met hers, his expression sombre. 'This thing with you and Lucas—is it for real? Are you and he together? A couple?'

She realised this was her chance to put an end to any false notions he might nurture about getting back with her. 'Yes,' she said. 'We've been together for some time now.'

'Since the wedding.' It was a flat statement.

'Yes.'

His mouth made a straight line. 'I suppose I should have known it was on the cards from the way he reacted back then. He'd had his eye on you all evening.'

Had he? Sophie was cautious. She had to be careful what she said to him, because she didn't want to risk messing this up. Once and for all, Nathan had to understand that there was no going back, but she wanted to let him down easily. 'Nathan, you know things hadn't been right between you and me for a long time, don't you? We were like chalk and cheese...but I... I'll always want you as a friend, a good friend…you have to know that. I hope we can still get along well together.'

He gave a rueful smile. 'Of course. Perhaps I've been in denial. I know I took you for granted, and I took over when instead I should have listened to what you had to say. I've learned my lesson, and I felt I had to keep trying to win you back. But I see now that it's all over.' He looked into her eyes. 'I'll be okay, Sophie. Don't worry about me.'

He looked around as Lucas headed towards the shed. 'I guess the fence is finished,' he murmured.

'Is everything okay in here?' Lucas enquired. He looked from one to the other.

'It's fine,' Nathan said. He glanced at Sophie. 'Jessie is pregnant. I'd say she's due to give birth some time towards the end of January. Other than that she seems very healthy.'

Sophie's jaw dropped in surprise. 'I had no idea. I didn't think she'd come into season. Besides, I thought she was too young.'

Nathan shook his head. 'It can happen any time

from the age of six months onwards. Fortunately, she's strong and she's been well looked after. Both she and George have good pedigrees, so that bodes well for milk yield and so on. You'll know when she's getting ready to give birth, because there will be some subtle changes in her shape, she'll become increasingly restless, maybe she'll paw at her bed, and she'll keep getting up and then she'll lie down again. Just give me a ring when you think things are starting to happen, and I'll come over.'

He gave Sophie a minute or two to get over that news, and then he added, 'As to the goose, there's nothing physically wrong with him. I think he's finally realised he's not making that much of an impression on the hens. I suggest you get a female, to keep him company.'

Sophie laughed. 'I must have been going around with my head in the clouds. How could I not have worked out what it was with Jessie or Ferdie?'

Lucas laid an arm around her shoulders. 'A lot's happened in these last few months, one way and another. I don't think you can blame yourself for that.'

'That's true,' Nathan said. 'Anyway, the hens are healthy enough, too. They don't get as many daylight hours in the winter, and that's why egg production goes down. You could instal some heat lamps on timers to compensate for the extra hours of winter darkness, if you want to keep them laying—though they should have a period of rest. Other than that, I'd suggest you feed them extra protein and add some nutritious crumbles to their diet for a while. I can let you have some.'

'I'll do that. Thanks, Nathan.'

He nodded. 'I'll leave a bag of feed with you.' He frowned. 'I should go. I have to get on—I've another call to make a few miles down the road.'

She guessed he didn't want to hang around, especially with Lucas there. She walked with him to his car and saw him off a short time later.

As he drove away flakes of snow began to fall from the sky. The children shrieked with excitement, dancing around and holding out their arms so that the soft flakes covered them. William tilted his face to catch the snowflakes and wrinkled his nose as the snow melted on his forehead and ran in small rivulets down his cheeks.

'I think we should go inside,' she suggested to Lucas, who nodded agreement.

'I need to wash up,' he murmured. 'And I think William and Emily could do with warming up for a while.'

'I'll make some hot drinks,' Sophie said, 'and a bit later on I'll get some food together.' She looked at him, her blue eyes intent. 'Thanks for repairing the fence for me. I was expecting a temporary fix, but you've made a perfect job of it. It's as good as new.'

'You're welcome. We can't have George running amok, can we? I saw what he did to the herbaceous garden, never mind the vegetables. It's a wonder he didn't make himself sick.'

'Oh, he's very selective,' Sophie said with a chuckle. 'He only chooses the very best.'

They all trooped into the kitchen and put their damp outer garments on a wooden rack around the Aga to dry. Sophie made drinks, and when the children had warmed up, they went off to the playroom to examine the toys.

Emily came back after a moment, holding a small pile of letters. 'I found these in the hall,' she said. 'I thought you might want to look at them. Mummy always asks me to get the post for her.'

'Thanks, Emily. That was thoughtful of you.' Sophie smiled at her and relieved her of the envelopes. She glanced through them, and her expression straightened.

'Problem?' Lucas asked. Emily danced back along the hall to the playroom.

'Not really.' She was studying the franking stamp on the envelope. 'It's a letter from the adoption agency.' She sat down at the kitchen table and turned the envelope over in her hands. Her heart started to beat heavily, a steady thump, thump, and she felt as though she'd been winded.

'Give yourself a minute,' Lucas suggested. 'Do you want more coffee?'

She nodded absently. 'Yes, please.'

'If you have any brandy, you might want a drop in it. You look as though you might need it.'

'I'm okay,' she said, breathlessness making her voice unsteady. She tore open the envelope. There was a single sheet of paper inside, with just a couple of typed paragraphs.

She scanned them quickly and then looked up

at Lucas, who was watching her closely. 'They say they have information for me about my natural parents, but I need to go and see someone at the agency.' She laid the letter down on the table with a shaking hand. 'I don't know if I'm up to it. I feel strange, all at once. I don't know what to do. It's such a big step to take.'

'Like I said before, you have to give yourself time. You don't have to rush into anything.'

She nodded. 'It's a lot to take in. A few months ago my life seemed to be running along smoothly. I was happy here on the farm with my parents, and I had no idea that just a short time later it would all fall apart, that I would start to question everything that had gone before.'

He frowned. 'I'm sure your parents loved you dearly. They must have been a warm and loving couple. You can see their handiwork in everything about this place. The animals all have places where they can be warm and sheltered from the cold, and great outdoor spaces where they can roam free. There are beautiful shrubs in the garden and ramblers on the walls of the house. Inside, everything has been well looked after, and they even preserved the toys that you played with as a child.'

He studied her, his grey eyes questioning. 'Why would they have done all that if they didn't love you and care for your well-being? Didn't they help you through medical school and encourage you along the way?'

She nodded. 'I know what you're saying is right. Deep down, perhaps I always knew it, but I was hurt and upset. When they died, it was as though I'd been abandoned, and I know that sounds strange, because they didn't have any control over what happened…but I just felt lost and alone, and then when I found out that they weren't my real parents, it was like a betrayal. I couldn't think straight.'

'Do you feel better about them now?'

'Yes, I think I do.' She frowned, looking at him with troubled blue eyes. 'When you were out there, sifting through your toolbox, I had this sudden memory of my father, doing odd jobs about the place. The slightest thing that went wrong, his toolbox would be out and he'd set to and fix it. I used to be so proud of him, the way he worked so hard. It was important to him that everything should be done properly, that the farm would be preserved for posterity. It was my mother's vision, too.'

'So how does that fit in with you wanting to put the place on the market? Wouldn't you be throwing away everything he worked for?'

'I suppose you're right.' She stood up and went over to the worktop. Everything was crowding in on her and she didn't know how to deal with it. 'I ought to think about preparing a meal,' she said distractedly. 'I expect the children will be hungry before too long. I'm not sure what to give them. Some vegetable soup, perhaps, and crusty rolls? I could do jacket potatoes, with cheese.'

'That sounds fine.' Lucas came to stand beside her. 'I'll give you a hand.'

'Thanks.' His nearness confused her. She was so conscious of his long body, of the warmth that came from him. She wanted to reach out and touch him, but something held her back.

'There's so much you could do, if you were to stay here,' he said.

She gave a small sigh. 'I don't know about that.

There's the upkeep, the maintenance and the expense, as well as my work at the hospital. I'm not struggling for money, but it all adds up to a lot of responsibility.'

'It wouldn't have to add to your workload. I can see great opportunities for the place. If I was the owner, I would expand what's already here.' Amusement played around his mouth. 'I don't want to be presumptive and impose my ideas on you, like Nathan, but there are all sorts of ways you could make money—which in turn would help to pay for the upkeep of the place.'

'Such as?'

'Well, first of all, you could open it up to visitors at certain times of the year. It doesn't have to interfere with the running of the farm or intrude on the house. You might offer pony rides for very young children—obviously the Shetlands won't carry children who are much above ten years old. Maybe there's someone in the village who would be qualified to give riding tuition. And I love the way the animals roam about freely around here. It adds to the hillbilly atmosphere, and that attracts people. I'm sure a pets' corner would go down well.'

She laughed. 'You're adding to my workload, not cutting it.' All the same, the idea appealed to her. 'Is that what your parents' farm is like?'

'Yes, pretty much. I'm sure you could bring in some older teenagers or part-timers from the village to supervise things. It shouldn't cost too much, and in the summer you would get a lot of visitors, I'm positive.'

She was thoughtful, turning it over in her mind. 'I can see it has a lot of potential. I don't know too much about that kind of thing, though. I'd need quite a bit of help to set it up.'

'My parents would give you all the help and advice you need. You should come and have dinner with us at the weekend and talk it over with them. I go over there quite often for Sunday lunch, and they've been asking me to bring you along. They're really pleased with the way you've helped out with William and Emily. In fact, they've asked if I will bring you along on Christmas Day, so that you can have Christmas dinner with us. Ella will be there, as well as Tom and the children.'

'I don't know,' she said, fidgeting a little. 'I'm not sure. What if they don't like me?'

He laughed and moved closer, giving her a hug. 'They'll love you. I'm absolutely certain of it. The children have been full of it, telling everyone all about you, and about the farm and the animals.'

She turned to face him, and his arms went around her, drawing her close. 'You have a strong, loving family, don't you?' she murmured. 'You're very fortunate.'

'I know I am. And I want you to share in that.' He smiled. 'I've fallen for you, big time, you know. I think it happened the very first day we met. You were an angel sent from heaven to earth, and you landed right in my lap. I couldn't believe my luck.'

He lowered his head and kissed her, a gentle, sweet, persuasive kiss that made her senses riot and instantly caused her blood pressure to go into overload. She wrapped her arms around his neck and clung to him, pressing her body against him, wanting desperately to be closer.

A muffled groan escaped him. 'Do you know what you're doing to me?' He ran his hand along the base of her spine and over the curve of her hip, easing her against his thighs. And all the time he was deepening the kiss, teasing her lips, making her burn with need, making her want everything he had to offer.

She ran her hands over his chest, loving the feel of him, tantalised by the way he rained kisses over her mouth, her cheeks, the smooth slope of her throat. His hand slid up over her rib cage, stopping to cup the soft fullness of her breast. 'You make me want you so much,' he said, his voice thick and muffled against her throat. 'I can't help thinking that you and I would be so good together.'

'I like the sound of that,' she whispered. His hand gently tested the weight of her breast, his thumb moving in slow circles that made her heart thud and caused her head to swim with a hunger that she had never known before.

He kissed her again, a passionate, demanding kiss that took her breath away. 'I hated seeing you with Nathan,' he said in a gruff tone. 'I wanted you for myself. I can't bear the thought of you with anyone else. I never thought this would happen, but I realise I don't want my freedom any more if it means I can't have you. I want to make you mine…only mine.'

He looked at her, the glitter of desire burning in his eyes. 'I'd hoped I want to be with you for always—I love you, Sophie. Do you think you could walk down the aisle with me one day? You'd make me the happiest man on earth if you said yes.'

She pulled in a shaky breath. 'It's what I want more than anything in the world,' she said softly. 'I love you, Lucas. I didn't know it to begin with, I didn't realise what was happening to me, and then all at once it struck me that I was lost without you.'

'I feel the same way. I feel as though we belong together—we have our whole lives ahead of us. I want to make you happy, to give you everything that you could possibly want—a family, maybe, to make up for all that you've lost. Everything I once believed in has been turned on its head since I met you, and I'm even beginning to think that children would make everything perfect. In time, who knows? We could start a loving, happy family of our own.'

'A family...' Something filtered through the hazy swirl of happiness that filled her head. The world seemed to tilt on its axis, and a feeling of anxiety washed through her, driving out all the joy that had been there. Something was terribly wrong, but she couldn't quite put a finger on what it was.

She wanted a family, more than anything. She longed to hear the sounds of children in the house—Lucas's children. Only, that wasn't going to be possible, was it? It would be utterly selfish of her to bring children into the world.

Her fingers stilled, coming to rest on the hard wall of his chest. 'I don't... I think... Lucas... I...' She looked up at him, her blue eyes blurring with a mist of tears. 'I can't...'

'What is it, Sophie? What are you trying to say?' He looked at her with love in his eyes, and she felt as though her heart was breaking.

'I can't marry you, Lucas. I can't marry you because it wouldn't be right.'

'What do you mean?'

'I can't. I daren't have children. I can't bring them into the world, knowing that they might inherit my genes—my defective genes. That's what the doctors are talking about, isn't it? An inherited disease? I don't want to put them through that, and I can't marry you, knowing how good you are with children, how much you care about them, knowing that you want a family some day. I wasn't thinking when I said that it was what I wanted. I'm so sorry.'

He looked at her, his face pale, his features suddenly tense, almost as though she had struck him. He was stunned, speechless, and she could see that there was a battle raging inside him.

'Shouldn't you let me decide whether or not children will make a difference?' he said at last, shaking his head as though to clear it. 'Even if you do have the disease, you can't know for certain that our children would become ill. If I'm not a carrier, then they couldn't get the disease.'

'But they could all be carriers, and that would affect them throughout their lives. It would cause them to be cautious about the choices they make.

I've looked into this very carefully, Lucas. I don't want to be responsible for burdening them with that.'

'You're just using that as an excuse,' he said tersely. 'Maybe you're afraid that something will go wrong if you allow yourself to love and be loved. You've been hurt, the people you loved have deserted you—or so you think. You're over-emotional, and perhaps you need more time—more space—so that you can think things through.'

He moved away from her, and for a second or two it felt as though he had abandoned her. She swayed slightly and held on to the worktop for support.

Then she saw that Emily had come into the room, with William following close behind her. Perhaps Lucas had seen them before she had.

'We're hungry,' they said in chorus. 'Can we have something to eat?'

Sophie nodded. Right then she couldn't trust herself to speak.

CHAPTER NINE

SINCE her fallout with Lucas, Sophie had decided to focus on her main priority—work. It didn't make it any easier, though, knowing that Lucas was so near yet he was holding himself so far from her. He'd spoken to her briefly, a few curt words, and she felt as though her world was falling apart. She'd scarcely seen anything of him this last week, and she had the horrible feeling he'd been avoiding her.

What else could she expect? He'd asked her to marry him and after she'd turned him down he had withdrawn from her completely and she didn't know how to handle that. It was upsetting, and all her deepest fears came to the fore. How could anyone love her when she was damaged… defective? Wasn't that ultimately what had caused the break-up with Nathan, because he hadn't been able to handle her emotional distress and her illness?

Now Lucas was reacting in the same way. 'Perhaps we both need time to think things through,' he'd said, and she didn't know where they could go from there. Was he right when he said she was afraid to love and be loved?

She tried to push these thoughts from her mind and concentrate instead on examing her patient. He was six years old, a fair-haired boy who was recovering from heart surgery that he'd undergone a couple of days ago.

'It's the day before Christmas Eve, Ryan,' she said quietly, 'and we want you well enough to go home for Christmas so we'd better sort out what's making you poorly, hadn't we?' She smiled at him. He was pale faced and worn out, his heart beating way too fast. He didn't have the strength to answer her just then.

She held the oxygen mask close to his nose and mouth so that he could get more oxygen into his lungs.

'Is he not responding to the treatment?' Lucas asked in a low voice, coming to stand beside her.

She shook her head. 'We'll have to wait and see if that last dose of adenosine works,' she told him. She glanced at him warily. ‘We haven’t had much chance to talk properly lately, have we?’

He shrugged. ‘We’ve been busy. It’s been a madhouse all week. I don’t think anyone realises it’s Christmas.’

‘No. Illness doesn’t take any account of that, does it?’ Though she doubted that was what had kept Lucas from seeking her out.

She looked at the monitors once more. There was no distinctive change in the readings and that worried her.

Then, just a few minutes later, the child’s heart rate began to spike again. He looked very poorly, breathless, and it was clear he wasn’t coping at all well with his rapid heart rate. She guessed he couldn’t go on much longer this way without collapsing. ‘I’ll give him propranolol and see if that will help.’

Lucas nodded, assisting with the oxygen while she prepared the medication. When it was done, she watched the child, her gaze moving from him to the monitors and back again.

‘We’ll have to give it a while and see what happens.’

She sent him a quick glance, but his expression remained closed. She checked the monitors once more.

'There's still no change,' she said. 'I think it's just a glitch stemming from the surgery and the anaesthetic in his system. I don't think it's going to be an ongoing problem, but we need to get it sorted.'

'You could try procainamide,' he suggested, and she nodded.

'I'll set up an infusion.' She started on it right away, too involved in her patient's care to worry right then about Lucas's curt manner. She faced another tense wait to see if this medication would work.

Lucas glanced around the ward. 'There don't seem to be as many children on the ward as usual, or is it my imagination?'

'You're right, there aren't. I've been doing lots of checks on all the children. I want to send as many of them home as I possibly can for Christmas. Some will be readmitted after Boxing Day, but if they're well enough, it gives them the chance to be with their families for a time.'

'That's good. It's great that you can do that,' Lucas said. 'I heard that a local theatre troupe is coming in this afternoon to do a pantomime for them. That should cheer everybody up.'

'Yes. Unfortunately, I won't be here to see it.'

'Why is that?'

'I've an appointment with the adoption agency this afternoon,' she told him, a worried look coming into her eyes.

'That's good, isn't it?' He gave her a puzzled look. 'I mean, at least you'll finally get to know who your parents are and what happened all those years ago.'

She frowned. 'I don't know. I'm a bit apprehensive about it, to be honest. I don't really know how I feel—sick, mostly, I think.'

She checked the monitor once more and gave a sigh of relief. Ryan's heart rate was at last beginning to slow down. 'That's good,' she murmured. 'He's coming out of it. Perhaps I can safely leave him in Hannah's hands now.'

She lightly stroked Ryan's hair and leaned closer to him so that he would be able to hear her. 'The medicine's working. You'll feel better soon, sweetheart,' she told him, and was rewarded with an almost imperceptible nod. 'Just rest, and Hannah will come and stay with you. Your mother will be here any minute now. She just went to phone your dad.'

She sent Lucas a quick sideways glance. 'Do you want to come with me to see Marcus off? I know you have a special interest in him. He's leaving us this morning.'

'Is he? That's brilliant news. He's made a good recovery, hasn't he?'

'Yes, he has.' She smiled. 'I'm really pleased for him. He's such a lovely, bright and bubbly little boy.'

Marcus was thrilled to bits to be going home. 'Look!' he exclaimed excitedly. 'I made you a card. There's a snowman on it, see? He's made from cotton wool, and I used red felt for the buttons. I cutted them out all by myself.'

'He's lovely.' Sophie gave Marcus a hug. 'And he has such a lovely smile. It's almost as lovely as yours.'

He giggled, and looked up at his mother, who was smiling fondly. 'He insisted on making it for you,' she said. 'The trouble we've had, keeping it secret!'

Sophie laughed. 'I shall miss you, Marcus,' she told him. 'But I'm so glad that you're feeling better and that you're well enough to go home.' He was all packed and ready, and now that Hannah had given him his package of medication, Sophie could discharge him. 'You go home and have a lovely Christmas,' she said.

She and Lucas watched him leave the ward with his mother and father. He was in a wheelchair, so as not tire him out, but it wouldn't be long before he was walking about under his own steam.

'You know,' Lucas said softly, 'there's a lesson to be learned there.'

She glanced at him, a question in her eyes, and he added, 'Marcus was born with something wrong with him, but you've just shown that it doesn't have to stay with him his whole life. There are ways round these things. You've learned how to manage your illness, through cutting things from your diet and maintaining a healthy regime. No matter what the reason, you said yourself, you're already beginning to feel better. Surely any children you might have who were born with the disease would discover it early and learn how to manage it before it ever became a problem?'

Her brow creased. 'I don't know.' She was in a quandary and she didn't know how to get out of it. 'I want to do the right thing. Doesn't everyone want their child to be born without any problems? Believe me, I've thought about it a lot this last week. I'm still waiting for the results of the genetic tests, but what if my GP turns out to be right? The ultrasound scan I had a couple of months ago showed there was a problem with my liver—they're not sure what caused it, but it's quite possible it's the disease.' She was still waiting on the results of a more recent scan.

He didn't answer, but his expression was solemn, and she guessed he'd been hoping for a different response. She glanced at him, not knowing how she could put things right, and instead she changed the subject, saying, 'How's Ella doing? Will she be home for Christmas?'

He nodded. 'Actually, she came home yesterday. Her blood pressure was back to normal, so with any luck things will go smoothly from now on. She's due to have the baby in a fortnight, so let's hope she stays calm over the holidays. My mother will be doing all the preparations for Christmas dinner and so on, and she's planning on having Ella and Tom stay over so that she can keep an eye on her. She wants Ella to have a good rest, and that seemed the best solution.'

'I'm glad she's okay. It's good that your mother's looking out for her.'

He looked at her closely. 'Look, Sophie, I'm off duty at three this afternoon. What time is your appointment at the adoption agency? Perhaps I could go with you and offer you some moral support. It's not the sort of thing you want to do on your own, is it?'

'No, that's true.' Her heart gave a small leap at his offer. 'It's at four o'clock. Are you sure you wouldn't mind coming with me? I feel such a wimp, and I don't know why I'm getting myself in such a state about it, but I think I'm a bit worried about how I might react when I get there and hear what they have to say.'

'I want to go with you.' His gaze met hers. 'I love you, Sophie. I've tried to keep my distance, but it doesn't make any difference. I still feel the same way. I'll be there for you always, whenever you need me.'

His words brought sudden tears to her eyes, and she blinked hard, trying to push them away. Why couldn't she give in to her deepest yearnings? She wanted to marry him, to be with him for ever, but every time she thought about it, this huge barrier came up and knocked her back. Would he really want to stay with her when he came to realise her illness would not go away? How would she cope if his feelings for her changed and he decided their relationship wasn't working?

'I don't deserve you,' she whispered. 'You're way too good for me. I'd thought maybe we should make a clean break of it, but I hate the thought of you not being around, of not seeing you or being with you. That's totally selfish of me, isn't it?'

He wrapped his arms around her. 'No, it isn't, not at all. I want to be with you...and no matter what's happened between us, I want you to come and spend Christmas with me at my parents' house. They want you to be there, too—so please say you'll come?'

She nodded. Why was she fighting him? It was so tiring. 'All right. I will.' How could she bear to spend Christmas away from him? Let them get the festive season over with and then maybe she could start to think more clearly about the future.

Lucas went back to A and E, leaving Sophie to check on her young patients. By tomorrow afternoon, Christmas Eve, she wanted as many children to be on their way home as was possible.

Lucas met up with her at half past three. 'All set?' he asked, and she nodded. 'Okay, then. Let's go.'

The agency had offices in a building in town. 'Dr Welland,' a woman from the agency greeted her, 'it's good to see you. I'm Grace Matthews. Please sit down, both of you.' She included Lucas in her smile.

Sophie sat down, and Lucas took the seat beside her. Perhaps he sensed her distress, because he reached out and laid his hand calmly over hers.

The warmth and unspoken message of support in that contact gave her courage.

'In your letter,' Sophie began, 'you said that you had information for me about my natural parents.'

Grace nodded. She opened a file and looked briefly through the documents in there. 'First of all, perhaps I should tell you that your father is still alive, and that he's willing for you to make contact with him if you should wish to do so.'

Sophie sharp intake of breath was audible. 'He's alive? Somehow I don't think I was expecting that.' She frowned. 'Does that mean my mother…?'

The woman's grey eyes were full of sympathy. 'Unfortunately, your mother died when you were a baby. You were about six months old at the time, I believe.'

Sophie sat straight backed in her chair, her whole body tense. 'Can you tell me what happened? Why was I put up for adoption if my father is still alive? Didn't he want me?' Lucas gently squeezed her hand, and she registered that silent gesture of comfort and made an effort to relax.

'I think your father wanted you very much,' Grace said. 'It appears that your parents went out to Africa when you were just a few months old. Apparently, your father worked all over the world on different projects, and clearly he was keen to have his family with him. Unfortunately, when they were in Africa, your mother was taken ill with some kind of fever that came on rapidly. She died within a matter of days.' She paused, giving Sophie time to take all that in.

'That must have been a dreadful shock for my father,' Sophie said in a quiet voice. 'How do you know all this?'

'It's in the notes that were made at the time of your adoption. Your father was worried that conditions over there might be dangerous for you, that you might succumb to a similar virus, and so he came back to England and arranged for you to be fostered. As I said, his job took him all over the world and I believe he was concerned about the responsibility of keeping a young baby with him.'

The woman removed a sheet of paper from the file and handed it to Sophie. 'He left this letter for you. Basically, he wanted you to know that he loved you very much and that having you adopted was a very difficult decision for him. He's made it clear that you can contact him at any time. He's left an address and phone number with us.'

Sophie's hand was shaking as she took the letter. Her father's writing was bold and black, and as the woman had said he seemed to be intent on explaining how he felt about leaving his child with foster-parents.

'I came back from time to time, from wherever in the world I'd been working,' her father wrote, 'and went to see how you were getting on with your foster-parents, the Wellands. They let me stay with them for several days at a time. You seemed to be so happy with them. You turned to them for everything, and after a while you started to call them Mummy and Daddy. It came so naturally to you, and they were so loving towards you in return that it almost broke my heart. I realised that I couldn't take you away from them and destroy the bond that had grown between you. You were safe and secure with them. So in the end I agreed to let them adopt you.

'I'll always love you, Sophie. You'll always be my daughter, and if you should ever want to get in touch with me and want to meet up with me, that would make me very, very happy.'

She handed the letter to Lucas so that he could read it. Tears began to roll slowly down her cheeks, and she brushed them away with the back of her hand, not knowing how to handle her pent-up emotions. Lucas offered her a clean, white handkerchief and said quietly, 'There's no shame in feeling the way you do. It's perfectly natural.'

'Yes, it is,' Grace said. 'Most people react the way you have. Give yourself a day or so to come to terms with the news, and then perhaps you might want to phone him or write him a letter.'

'How do you know his address and phone number are the right ones?' Sophie asked. 'This all happened many years ago.'

Grace smiled. 'He gets in touch with us once a year just to see if we've heard from you. He always makes sure we have his current contact number.' She handed Sophie a card with the details printed on it. 'Take that with you…and good luck.'

Sophie and Lucas left the agency sometime later and walked slowly back to Lucas's car.

'Your father sounds like a man who wants the best for you,' he said. 'It must make you feel good, knowing that he cares so much.'

'Yes, it does.' She turned to face him. 'I'm so relieved that you were there with me at the agency. I don't think I could have gone through it without you.'

'And I won't be able to get through these next few days without you,' he murmured. 'I'm glad you're going to be with me over Christmas. You know I want to persuade you to change your mind and give me the answer I want to hear, don't you? I'm not going to give up, Sophie. I meant it when I said I need you.'

She pulled in a shaky breath. 'You might change your mind about that once you realise what it will mean for you, being with me, and how it will affect your life. Let's get through Christmas, at least, and then we'll try to work out how we go on from there. I don't know how else to deal with this, Lucas. It's much too painful.'

CHAPTER TEN

SOPHIE looked out of her bedroom window on Christmas morning and saw that everything around was once more covered with a blanket of snow. It was beautiful, the branches of the trees edged thickly with white, the rooftops pristine and glistening. The bird table and birdbath were outlined with frost, and icicles hung from the timbers.

Lucas would be calling for her at any moment. It was still early, but he'd said he wanted to take her over to his parents' house in time for breakfast. She was excited, and at the same time a little apprehensive. Would his family take to her? But above all she wanted to see Lucas and to be with him.

He rang the doorbell a moment later, and she hurried downstairs to greet him. 'Hi,' he said, stopping briefly to look her over. Flame kindled in his smoke-grey eyes. 'You're gorgeous. It never fails to amaze me how lovely you are… I just can't get enough of you.'

He swept her into his arms and kissed her soundly. 'Happy Christmas, Sophie,' he murmured against her cheek. 'I know mine is all the better for having you with me.'

'Happy Christmas,' she said in return, her eyes sparkling with joy at being in his arms once more. So she was living dangerously but what did it matter? She would take these precious moments and store them in her heart for ever. What harm could it do to take the good things life had to offer, just for once?

In her pocket, she had a letter that Dr Mason must have pushed through her letterbox yesterday evening, on his way back from doing his house calls. She hadn't been able to bring herself to open it. It must surely contain the results of the tests she'd had done at the hospital and she didn't want to risk spoiling these next few days by reading them.

'We're all set for breakfast at the house,' he said, helping her into his car a few minutes later.

'I expect it'll be a take-us-as-you-find-us affair, though, because everything's in chaos at home and my dad's been left to generally organise things.'

'Has he? Is your mother all right?' She sent him an oblique glance as he slid into the driver's seat and started the car's engine. His car was a solid, top-of-the-range saloon, designed to cope easily with the hazards of icy roads. 'Does your mother need some help? I must be putting her out, arriving so early. There's always so much to do on Christmas Day, with the dinner to prepare, and so on. I don't want to put your parents out in any way.'

'It isn't that… Ella went into labour late last night, and everything's been turned upside down ever since. She wanted Mum to be with her at the hospital, as well as Tom, and of course my mother was desperate to be there. She was with her when William and Emily were born, and this one's no exception.'

'So is she still at the hospital?'

He shook his head. 'She came back to grab some clothes for Ella and the baby. They weren't expecting her to go into labour for another two weeks, so they didn't have an overnight bag prepared. I know she wants to get back to Ella as soon as possible, but she wanted to meet you, too.' He smiled. 'I said I'd get you there as soon as possible.'

He was as good as his word. They pulled up in the driveway of his parents' farmhouse just a short time later, and any worries that Sophie might have had about his parents' reaction to her disappeared with the opening of the front door.

'Sophie,' his mother said, 'I'm so pleased to meet you. I've been waiting for this day for such a long time. Lucas has told us so much about you.' She was an attractive woman, with soft brown hair framing an oval face and green eyes that were alive with friendly curiosity. Jessica Blake had a natural ability to make friends. Her openness and good nature shone through.

'We're all over the place here,' Samuel Blake greeted her, 'but you mustn't take any account of that. Make yourself at home and bear with us, if you will. We're usually much better organised, but with Ella in hospital it's turned everything on its head.' He was tall and dark haired, with grey eyes that were very much like his son's.

'Well, maybe there's something I can do to help,' Sophie ventured, stepping into the hall. 'I don't want to get in the way, but if there's anything I can do, you just have to say.'

They all went through to the kitchen, a big, square room with golden oak units all around and a table to one side where knives and forks were laid out in place settings, ready for breakfast.

'Sit yourselves down,' Jessica said, going over to the cooker and helping her husband with the pans. 'It's been such a hoo-ha this morning. I'm afraid dinner is going to be very late. That's why I'm doing a fry-up now. We have to keep the hunger pangs at bay somehow.'

She served up bacon and eggs, along with tomatoes and beans, and said on a musing note, 'I'm just not sure when I'll be able to get started with it. Ella's expecting me back at the hospital any time soon. And there's no point in me leaving Sam to see to the turkey. That would be a disaster.' She exchanged wry glances with her husband. 'He's a lovely man, but absolutely hopeless with anything more than toast or scrambled eggs.'

'You'll see that the toast is cooked to perfection,' Sam pointed out, waving a hand towards the toast rack. 'Golden brown, edge to edge… perfect.' His eyes twinkled with amusement. 'Help yourselves. There's marmalade, and apricot or raspberry preserve, too.'

'This is all wonderful,' Sophie said appreciatively. 'It's much more than I expected, especially with so much going on here today.' She was thoughtful as she speared the golden yolk of a perfectly cooked egg. 'You know, there's no reason why I couldn't cook Christmas dinner for you, and then you could relax and be with Ella as much as you want. I'm not sure quite how I'd manage with a strange cooker, though, so you wouldn't have to expect perfection—I'm used my Aga and all its idiosyncrasies.'

'I couldn't ask you to do that.' Jessica was obviously thrown by the suggestion, but Sophie guessed there was a hint of something else. Relief, perhaps?

'It's no trouble,' Sophie said. 'Really, I mean it.'

'We could take everything over to Woodvale, to Sophie's place,' Lucas suggested. 'Then she could use the Aga. I'll give her a hand with everything, and you and Dad can relax. It's not every day you get to have a new grandchild.'

Jessica drew in a quick breath and looked at her husband, who lifted a dark brow just a fraction, and said, 'That makes sense to me.'

'Then that's all settled,' Lucas said. 'We'll head off, just as soon as we've finished eating, and then we can get started.' He glanced at Sophie, and she nodded.

'I'm just glad I decided to decorate for Christmas after all,' she murmured.

'Were you not going to bother this year?' Jessica was sympathetic. 'I know you've had a lot of troubles lately.'

'That's right.' Sophie smiled. 'But in the end I decided to go ahead with it after all. It was a tradition with my parents, and I realised it was one I needed to keep going.'

'I'm sure things will turn out just fine for you,' Jessica said, patting her hand. She glanced at her son. 'Lucas will make sure of that.'

Sophie's expression was rueful. If only it were as simple as that.

Lucas, though, did everything he could to live up to his mother's prediction. He loaded up the car with all the makings of Christmas dinner, and within the hour they were on the road back to Sophie's farm.

'I'll sort out the vegetables,' he said, once they had unloaded everything into her farmhouse kitchen. 'Do you need a hand with the turkey?'

She shook her head. 'I'll be fine with it,' she murmured. Then she smiled. 'It's certainly a big one, isn't it? I think your mother must have reckoned on feeding everyone in the neighbourhood.'

Lucas laughed. 'She's not one to do things by halves, my mother.'

They worked together companionably in the warm kitchen, and before too long the wonderful aroma of slow-roasted turkey and chestnut stuffing began to fill the air.

'I think we've done everything we can for now,' Sophie said. 'I've set the table in the dining-room, so everything is more or less ready in there. Have you seen it? It looks good, don't you think?'

She led the way to the dining-room, going to stand to one side of the magnificent stone fireplace, where a fire burned and logs crackled, throwing up orange flames.

Lucas cast his glance over the long table. 'I think it looks great, with the red and gold Christmas crackers and the berries and fir-cone centrepiece. That's a great touch. And you've made a good job of the decorations in here, too.' He looked around at the glittering Christmas bells and silver stars that hung at intervals from the ceiling. There was a green garland over the fireplace, with shiny holly leaves and bright red berries, and in a corner of the room stood a fir tree, hung with gleaming baubles that reflected the light from the fire.

He became thoughtful all at once. 'Of course, there is one thing that's missing.'

Sophie frowned. 'What is it? Have I forgotten something?' She was worried all at once.

He shook his head. 'I have it. It's in one of the boxes I brought in from the car. It's in the corner, beneath the Christmas tree.'

She looked at the large box wrapped up in

colourful Christmas paper. 'I wondered what that was. I thought perhaps it was a present for your parents.'

'No, it's something for you. I thought we could we could make good use of it today.' He went over there and lifted it up, bringing it back to her and placing it down on the polished wooden sideboard. 'Open it,' he suggested.

She carefully unwrapped the packaging, opening up the box. Lifting layers of bubble wrap out of the way, she revealed a glint of crystal. 'Oh...' she said on a soft gasp, 'it's my crystal punch bowl. And it looks perfect.' She turned to look at him. 'But how...?'

'I took it to a glass restorer,' he murmured. 'The damage was confined to the top of the bowl, so he was able to file away the chipped edges. Then, apparently, he bevelled the crystal rim and adjusted the fluting to make it as near perfect as possible.'

'He's made such a good job of it you'd never know it had been broken.' She shook her head. 'I don't know what to say. I'm overwhelmed.' Tears sprang into her eyes and she tried to blink them away. 'This was so thoughtful of you. I thought you'd forgotten all about it.'

'I couldn't do that, knowing how much it meant to you.' He smiled. 'I'll fill it up for you in a while, and I think it should have pride of place here, on the sideboard, don't you?'

She nodded, wiping away the dampness from her cheeks. He wrapped his arms around her. 'That's not all,' he said. 'I do have something else for you, and I want you to think carefully before you try to refuse it.'

He put a hand in his trousers pocket and produced a small, gift-wrapped box.

'Is that what I think it is?' Sophie whispered. 'You know I—'

He placed a finger gently over her lips. 'Listen to what I have to say first, please. Will you promise me that…that you'll listen?'

Her blue eyes were troubled, but she nodded silently.

'Good.' He pulled in a quick breath. 'Look, I know I said that I wanted children some day, but it's not the be all and end all—'

'I couldn't make you go back on what you

want,' Sophie cut in. 'I would hate myself if you did that, and in time you might come to resent me for denying you what you really want.'

He drew her closer and silenced her with a gentle kiss on her soft lips. 'I hadn't finished,' he said. 'Just supposing it does turn out that you have the disease, there are alternatives we could consider.'

'But none that take away the fact that our children might be carriers.'

He slid the box back into his pocket. 'That's true…but what's the possibility that they would meet and marry another carrier? Very low, I would have thought.' He frowned. 'The other possibility is that we could have IVF treatment. That way, the embryos would be screened for the disease, and so there would be no danger of us having a child that is either a carrier or a sufferer.'

'I didn't think there were any centres locally that would do that.'

He shrugged. 'Distance doesn't really matter, does it? And what about adoption? You were shocked to find out that you were adopted because you discovered the truth too late—but don't you see that you could give another child the same gift that your adoptive parents gave you? All I'm saying is that we have choices, and we don't have to make up our minds right now. Just remember that you're feeling so much better now. You're not getting nearly so many pains in your joints, and that's a really good sign. You're basing your decisions on the way you felt some months ago. Who knows? By next spring or summer, you'll be feeling on top of the world and you'll wonder why you ever had any doubts.'

Sophie ran her fingertips lightly over his chest. 'I'm so weak-willed,' she said. 'I love you so much and I want to do the right thing, but when I'm with you all I can think about is that I never want to leave you.'

'Then don't. You've been honest with me, straightforward, and I know the score. Let me make the decision about how I want to handle my life from here on.' He kissed her tenderly, lovingly, drawing from her a shaky sigh. 'I want to marry you, Sophie,' he said. 'Please say that you'll marry me.'

She laid her head against his chest. 'Are you sure it will be all right?' she said in a hesitant voice.

'I'm positive.'

She looked up at him, and in that moment, seeing the sincerity in his grey eyes, seeing the love that was written there, she wondered why she had ever held back. Between them, they could make things work, couldn't they?

'Then I will,' she said softly. 'I will marry you.' She gave him a rueful smile. 'I hope you know what you're doing.'

'Of course I do. I've wanted you since the first moment I set eyes on you, and I've grown to love you along the way. I couldn't imagine life without you. Things will work out well for us, I know it.'

She smiled up at him, her lips parting for his kiss, and for a while there was no sound in the room except for the logs crackling in the hearth and the soft whisper of the decorations as they drifted lightly in the warm air currents.

'I love you, Lucas,' she whispered, some time later, looking up at him and winding her arms around his neck. 'You make me feel so good—you've been there for me through everything.'

'That's how it will always be,' he said softly.

She kissed him gently, and then eased back from him, taking a deep breath. 'Perhaps this is the time for me to open my letter,' she said, faint reluctance in her voice.

'What letter?'

'From my GP. It was pushed through my letterbox last night. I haven't had the courage to open it until now. Shall I do it or should I leave it until after Christmas is over?'

'Lord, no. Open it now.' He gave a wry smile. 'I wouldn't have the willpower to wait that long. Read it now, while I'm with you, and if it's bad news I'm here to help you through it.'

'All right.' She pressed her lips together briefly and then pulled the envelope from her pocket.

There were several sheets of paper inside. One was a letter from Dr Mason, saying, 'I only received these test results this morning, Sophie, and I thought you would want to have them as soon as possible. Basically, the results of the genetic tests are negative, which means you don't have the disease, neither are you a carrier. Secondly, the recent ultrasound scan of your liver shows that things are pretty much back to normal.

'The specialist and I have come to the conclusion, from looking at your blood test results, that you had a viral infection that caused problems with your liver, which in turn affected your body's ability to use iron. Now that the virus has cleared up, your liver is returning to its former healthy state, and the iron stores in your body are gradually being released from your tissues, so that your aches and pains should disappear within a few weeks.

'I'm sure this is will put your mind at rest, Sophie. Enjoy your Christmas.'

She passed the letter to Lucas. 'It's good news,' she told him, her face breaking into a smile. 'The very best Christmas present I could have hoped for.'

He read the letter and scanned the papers showing the test results. 'I'm so glad for you, Sophie. To think you've gone through all that worry and now at last it's all over.' He put the letter down on a low table. 'You can't imagine how happy I am for you…for us.'

His arms circled her once more, and he kissed her, tenderly, with all the love and passion that was pent up inside him. Sophie clung to him, kissing him in return, her heart filled with joy.

'As for Christmas presents…I'd almost forgotten…' he murmured against her cheek some minutes later. He moved back from her a fraction, and took the small box from his pocket once more. 'Not exactly a Christmas present,' he said as he handed it to her. 'It's more a once-in-a-lifetime and forever kind of present.'

She undid the gift-wrapping and opened the lid of the box. Nestled on a bed of velvet was the most beautiful diamond ring she had ever seen. She gave a small gasp. 'Lucas…it's lovely. How did you…? I mean, it's perfect.'

'Are you sure?' He looked anxious, as though he hadn't been certain of her reaction. 'It comes as part of a pair. There's a wedding ring that goes along with it, engraved in the same way, but I thought if you didn't like it we could go and choose one together. It's just that this one leapt out at me. I thought it was exquisite, beautiful, like you. I really wanted you to have it.'

'It's absolutely the loveliest ring I've ever seen. I'm overwhelmed.'

He smiled, and carefully took the ring from her, placing it on the third finger of her left hand. 'That's where it belongs,' he said. 'For always.'

He kissed her again, and for some time they were wrapped up in each other, thinking of nothing but these precious moments in each other's arms. And then the silence was disturbed by the sound of a car drawing up outside and children's voices came excitedly from the driveway.

Lucas sighed. 'I guess there's no peace for the wicked,' he murmured. 'Christmas has arrived. We'd better get on with it.'

'Hi, Sophie, hi, Uncle Lucas!' William exclaimed, bursting into the house a moment later and coming to find them in the dining room. 'Mummy's had a baby. She's all tiny and pink faced and her skin's ever so soft. I kissed her and she made a funny shape with her mouth, like this…' He made a rosebud shape, opening and closing his mouth slightly. Then he looked around the room and spied the Christmas tree in the corner. 'Oh, you've got a tree with lots of baubles. There's a Santa one and a sparkly bell. I wonder if it rings?' He ran over to the tree and started to test out his theory.

'She's a lovely little baby,' Emily said thoughtfully. 'I like having a sister, but I guess a brother would have been all right after all. William *can* be quite funny.' She went after her brother, standing with him to inspect the ornaments on the tree.

'They're full of it.' Jessica chuckled, taking off her coat and shaking the flakes of snow from her hair. 'We've left Tom and Ella together to enjoy their new little bundle.' She laughed. 'I did ask if they wanted me to bring them some Christmas dinner, but neither of them seemed to care what day it was.'

'So now we're back and ready to give you a hand,' Sam said, looking from Sophie to Lucas and back again. 'Are you two all right? You're looking a bit flushed.'

'Uh...I guess we've been standing a bit too close to the fire,' Lucas improvised, casting a quick glance in Sophie's direction. She tried to hide a smile. 'Anyway, I have to get on with making some punch,' he said. 'We've a glorious crystal bowl just crying out to be filled.'

'Ah, well, I've just the thing for that,' his father said, looking to where the glittering punch bowl had pride of place on the sideboard. 'I've brought some drink along with me…cider, brandy, some fruit juices…you name it. We'll have fun mixing up a storm, won't we?'

Jessica looked over at Sophie and smiled. 'I'll give you a hand with the dinner, shall I? There are some wonderful smells coming from the kitchen.'

It was about an hour later when they sat down to dinner. The turkey was cooked to perfection, basted to a golden brown and cut into thick, smooth slices that melted in the mouth. Lucas sat next to Sophie, and everything was just as she could have wished. The food disappeared in good time, and there was a lot of laughter around the table as people pulled crackers and read out the jokes and the children played with the novelties.

'I got a whistle,' William announced, and proceeded to deafen everybody with shrill bursts of sound, until his sister persuaded him to swap it for a metal puzzle.

Lucas's mother went to fetch the Christmas pudding. It was steaming hot, topped with a sprig of holly and surrounded with a sauce made from lush, ripe berries.

She carefully served out each portion, handing the dishes around the table one by one and then offering whipped cream to be spooned over the appetising dessert.

'Jessica's home-made Christmas pudding is out of this world,' Sam said, tucking in. 'I sometimes think it's how she got me to marry her, plying me with plum pudding and all sorts of goodies.' He chuckled, his gaze meeting Jessica's.

'Oh, yes? Is that how come you kept inviting yourself to dinner? It wasn't me you wanted but my cooking.'

Sophie ate her pudding and then spluttered quietly as her teeth closed on something hard. Her eyes widened and she turned to look at Lucas by her side.

'Uh-oh. Sophie's found the silver piece,' he said, a smile playing over his mouth.

'You have to make a wish,' Jessica and Sam said in chorus.

Sophie put the shiny silver coin on the side of her plate and closed her eyes. There was only one thing she could possibly wish for...that she and Lucas would live happily ever after, and that all their children would be healthy and strong.

She made her wish and then opened her eyes and looked at Lucas. 'I can guess what you wished for,' he said. 'I can read it in your eyes. Everything will be just perfect, you'll see.' He reached for her and she laid her hand in his palm, so that the diamond ring sparkled under the overhead lights.

'Oh...' Jessica gasped with delight. 'Is there something we should know?'

'Definitely,' Lucas said, his voice filled with pride. 'Sophie's agreed to be my wife and I've promised her that from here on we're going to have a wonderful life together. I just know it's going to be perfect.'

* * * * *

Mills & Boon® Large Print Medical

May

THE CHILD WHO RESCUED CHRISTMAS	Jessica Matthews
FIREFIGHTER WITH A FROZEN HEART	Dianne Drake
MISTLETOE, MIDWIFE...MIRACLE BABY	Anne Fraser
HOW TO SAVE A MARRIAGE IN A MILLION	Leonie Knight
SWALLOWBROOK'S WINTER BRIDE	Abigail Gordon
DYNAMITE DOC OR CHRISTMAS DAD?	Marion Lennox

June

NEW DOC IN TOWN	Meredith Webber
ORPHAN UNDER THE CHRISTMAS TREE	Meredith Webber
THE NIGHT BEFORE CHRISTMAS	Alison Roberts
ONCE A GOOD GIRL…	Wendy S. Marcus
SURGEON IN A WEDDING DRESS	Sue MacKay
THE BOY WHO MADE THEM LOVE AGAIN	Scarlet Wilson

July

THE BOSS SHE CAN'T RESIST	Lucy Clark
HEART SURGEON, HERO...HUSBAND?	Susan Carlisle
DR LANGLEY: PROTECTOR OR PLAYBOY?	Joanna Neil
DAREDEVIL AND DR KATE	Leah Martyn
SPRING PROPOSAL IN SWALLOWBROOK	Abigail Gordon
DOCTOR'S GUIDE TO DATING IN THE JUNGLE	Tina Beckett

August

SYDNEY HARBOUR HOSPITAL: LILY'S SCANDAL	Marion Lennox
SYDNEY HARBOUR HOSPITAL: ZOE'S BABY	Alison Roberts
GINA'S LITTLE SECRET	Jennifer Taylor
TAMING THE LONE DOC'S HEART	Lucy Clark
THE RUNAWAY NURSE	Dianne Drake
THE BABY WHO SAVED DR CYNICAL	Connie Cox

September

FALLING FOR THE SHEIKH SHE SHOULDN'T	Fiona McArthur
DR CINDERELLA'S MIDNIGHT FLING	Kate Hardy
BROUGHT TOGETHER BY BABY	Margaret McDonagh
ONE MONTH TO BECOME A MUM	Louisa George
SYDNEY HARBOUR HOSPITAL: LUCA'S BAD GIRL	Amy Andrews
THE FIREBRAND WHO UNLOCKED HIS HEART	Anne Fraser

October

GEORGIE'S BIG GREEK WEDDING?	Emily Forbes
THE NURSE'S NOT-SO-SECRET SCANDAL	Wendy S. Marcus
DR RIGHT ALL ALONG	Joanna Neil
SUMMER WITH A FRENCH SURGEON	Margaret Barker
SYDNEY HARBOUR HOSPITAL: TOM'S REDEMPTION	Fiona Lowe
DOCTOR ON HER DOORSTEP	Annie Claydon

0412 LP 2P P2 Medical